He looked down a moment and then closely at her.

"Ruth, life's not always what it seems. I. . ." He appeared uncomfortable. "I can't say more, but just remember that. Please." His eyes pleaded with her. "I've got to go. Thanks for your help."

At least he's uncomfortable for being such a flirt and leading me on, Ruth thought. *Life sure wasn't what it seemed around him. Maybe he was seeing this woman all along, and I was just a diversion. How could I be so dumb?* She looked down at the paper. *In this small community I can't avoid him. I can't quit the war work. It's too important.*

She walked out the door and toward the car, where her grandparents waited. *Just push it all away, Ruth, and grow up, just as you tell your students to do when they have a hopeless crush on someone.*

JOAN CROSTON was born in Oregon, the setting of her first novel, *C for Victory*, but she currently lives in Missouri where she and her husband are restoring a 100-year-old farmhouse. They have two married daughters. "To me good Christian fiction is theology in action," Joan says. "In experiencing the lives of fictional characters, I live the Christian life the author portrays, and when I'm done I carry some of that Christian living away with me. That's the experience or message I would like to leave my readers."

C for
Victory

Joan Croston

Heartsong Presents

To my husband Lee; my daughters and sons-in-law, Kelly and Darren Kalthoff, Jenna and Erich Harris; and my friend Jan Shy. Thanks for your help, encouragement, and proof-reading—and for keeping me from being devoured by the computer!

A note from the author:
I love to hear from my readers! You may correspond with me by writing: **Joan Croston**
Author Relations
PO Box 719
Uhrichsville, OH 44683

ISBN 1-57748-983-7

C FOR VICTORY

Cover illustration by Chris Cocozza.

PRINTED IN THE U.S.A.

one

Ruth Sinclair tucked a strand of wavy brown hair under the red-and-white bandanna tied around her head and slipped into her coat. "Can you believe it, Grandma? The Nakamuras forced from their home! Raw egg thrown all over it—inside and out! How can anyone be so hateful?" She grimaced and gave a shudder. "Cleaning up the slimy mess over there is an awful job, but if you let it dry, it sticks like glue!"

Alma Peterson chuckled as she put the last of the dishes away. "Getting squeamish on us, Ruth?" she teased and hung up the dish towel.

"I didn't mean it that way, Gram," Ruth answered softly. "Cleaning up the mess is nothing compared to what the Nakamuras are going through."

Alma shut the cupboard door with a sigh. "And it's certainly no laughing matter, either. A community couldn't ask for better neighbors than the Nakamuras and then to treat them like this! Shipped off to an internment camp by the government and their home ransacked by hoodlums!" She shook her head as she grabbed the broom and tackled a dusting of flour that lay like a skiff of snow on the brick-patterned linoleum.

A cold spring wind whistled and whined around the corners of the old farmhouse. Inside, Alma's kitchen was warm and cozy as a fire crackled in the wood cookstove, and the fragrant aroma from her morning's baking lingered in the air.

Ruth buttoned her coat and glanced at the familiar clutter. A flour sifter and measuring cups waiting to be put away. Oatmeal cookies and loaves of fresh bread set out to cool. She smiled, remembering how a cookie and a hug had soothed her hurts over the years. *But that won't be enough comfort in this war,* she thought sadly.

She reached for a cookie, then paused as a plaintive moo drifted into the kitchen. A moment of silence followed, and it started again. "If it's not one thing, it's another," she sighed and stepped to the window to check on the heifer standing in the backyard. "I've chased that cow all over the place till I see hamburgers every time I look at it!"

"You'd better go before she wanders off, Ruth." Alma came up behind her and peered over her shoulder. "Grandpa's working at the back of the Nakamuras' house, replacing more of the windows those hoodlums broke. Tell him he needs to hurry home and get that cow back in the pasture. She won't mind anyone but him." She rested her broom against the wall and picked up the dustpan.

Ruth nodded and patted her coat for the Nakamuras' key, finally finding it in the pocket of the brown slacks she wore. "While I'm there, I'll stay and do more scrubbing, Gram. At least the kitchen's done. That was the worst. All those broken dishes!"

"Just do what you can, dear. The Ladies Aid will be out next week to finish cleaning." Alma emptied the dustpan and hurried to assemble a package of cleaning supplies.

Ruth picked up a cookie. "How can this be happening in America, Gram? Since Japan attacked Pearl Harbor, I know people are afraid, but we can't start turning on each other."

Alma handed her the supplies and patted her shoulder. "People aren't trusting the Lord, Ruth. They've let fear get ahold of them."

Ruth opened the door and stepped out to see the fawn-colored Jersey staring at her across the lawn. "Just wait. Grandpa'll take care of you!" she threatened. It bellowed and gave a frisky leap as she descended the steps.

Alma followed Ruth out on the wooden porch, wiping her hands on her blue-flowered apron. "I'll keep an eye on her till he gets here. At least she's happy with the grass in the yard for now."

Ruth hurried down the driveway and turned onto the gravel road, stepping carefully to avoid puddles left by the night's rain. She shuddered as the April wind tore at her coat, then whipped through the Douglas fir trees swaying beside the road.

Ahead, the Nakamuras' white farmhouse stood silent and empty against the gray sky. "It looks as gloomy as something out of a Gothic novel." She stared at the house as the wind tugged at her bandanna. "Lord, what's happening to our world?" she whispered.

Since the past December 7, when Japan had bombed Pearl Harbor, nothing had been the same. Lives had been disrupted as men went off to war and families moved to work in the war industry. Fear stalked everyone. As a result, the government had issued Executive Order Number 9066, requiring that all persons in America of Japanese ancestry be sent to internment camps. People were afraid the Japanese Americans might spy or signal the enemy. When a Japanese submarine fired on a petroleum complex near Santa Barbara, California, on February 23, their worst fears seemed to be confirmed. Though no evidence was found, fear pointed to spies and Japanese espionage.

She turned off the road and started up the driveway to the house with a sigh. "I wonder where they are n—"

A car roared up behind her and screeched to a halt. She whirled around to see an old battered car idling on the roadway. The driver thrust his head out the window, his face an angry red above a black, scraggly beard. He shook his fist in the air as he screamed at her. "We don't need no Jap lovers around here, Teach!" he shouted. "We drove them traitors off this place. Git back home and decide which side of this war yer on!" He gunned the engine, and the car sped down the road, careening around the bend and disappearing from view.

Ruth stood stunned. "Who was that?" she whispered. Her heart raced and prickles of fear ran down her arms. In the distance, she could hear a car coming toward her. She caught her breath. "I hope he's not coming back!" Quickly she turned down the muddy driveway.

She took a step and glanced toward the sound. As her shoe hit the slippery mud, her feet flew out from under her, and she fell backwards, catching herself on her hands. "Oh, no! Fine time to be clumsy, Ruth Sinclair!" she moaned aloud as she glanced up to see a late-model green Plymouth driving toward her. *At least it's not him,* she thought with relief. But what a place for the local teacher to be on display! She made a futile effort to stand, muttering at the mud covering her shoes and coat.

As the car reached the driveway, it suddenly swerved to the side of the road, skidding on the gravel till it came to a halt. The door flew open and a tall, well-built man jumped out. A quick jolt of fear ran through her as she stared at him.

"Are you all right, ma'am?" the stranger called out over the top of the car with an air of friendly concern.

Ruth could only nod. She looked carefully at the dark-haired stranger and hesitated. He was well dressed in a business suit and topcoat. Not the type to be a threat. "Just stuck in the mud," she finally answered.

The man stepped carefully to the driveway and reached out to pull her up. "No, my hands are too muddy," she protested. "You're dressed up. I can make it." She attempted to stand and slipped back down.

He smiled warmly, his dark brown eyes showing the hint of a tease. "When a lovely lady keeps falling at my feet, the least I can do is help her up. Here, grab hold. I'm washable." He pulled her to her feet and handed her a handkerchief to wipe her hands.

"Hey! You! What's going on out there?" George Peterson rushed around the corner of the farmhouse, a pitchfork in his hands. "You okay, Ruth?" he called out as he hurried toward them. He eyed the stranger warily, holding the fork in front of him.

She nodded and took a deep breath. "I slipped on the mud, Grandpa. This gentleman stopped to help me." She shook some of the mud off her shoes. "Did you hear what that man shouted? The one who roared by in that old car?"

George lowered the pitchfork, his eyes still on the stranger. "Heard it clear back there."

The man kept his eyes on the fork and stepped back to the edge of the road, one hand jingling the coins in his pocket. "I saw the lady had slipped on the mud, sir, and only stopped to give her a hand."

He let out his breath as George jabbed the pitchfork into the ground and said, "Appreciate that."

"Did something else happen here?" the stranger asked, glancing from Ruth to George with a puzzled look on his face.

Ruth related the incident. "I didn't recognize the man," she concluded.

George thrust a hand in the pocket of his overalls and turned to the stranger. "This is the Nakamura farm. We're neighbors. Promised to look after their place while they're gone." He leaned on the pitchfork but kept his eye on the stranger.

Anger flared in Ruth's eyes. "Can you believe it? The Nakamuras were hauled away with two days' notice. No trial. No checking their loyalty to this country. Just because they're of Japanese ancestry. They're American citizens, but it didn't mean a thing! They were appalled at Pearl Harbor." She sighed as her angry tirade cooled.

The stranger watched her intently and smiled. "The world sure could use more like you, ma'am." He reached up quickly as the wind tugged at his hat.

"We're cleaning up the damage so the place will be ready when they come home," she explained. "As soon as the government finds out they're loyal citizens, they should be released. After all, this is America." She lifted a muddy shoe. It sloshed and she smiled sheepishly. "Looks like I'm the one who needs to clean up."

"A mud bath's supposed to keep a lady beautiful." The man winked at her. "Don't mean to be impolite, but I'm late for an appointment." He opened his car door and turned. "Be careful, both of you. Anti-Japanese sentiment is strong right now. Too many people think every Japanese helped plan the attack on Pearl Harbor personally. And they don't take kindly to those who befriend them." He touched his hat as he climbed into the car and drove off.

George pulled the pitchfork out of the ground. "Don't remember seeing him around here before." He looked at Ruth's muddy appearance. "You'd better go clean up, and I'll get back to work. Nak and Suzi were good friends and neighbors. Those hoodlums won't scare us off."

"Oh, no, Grandpa; I almost forgot. Grandma needs you at home. A cow got out, and we couldn't get it back in the pasture."

George sighed. "That's Britches again. Too smart for her own britches!" He chuckled and winked at her. "You staying here?"

Ruth nodded and retrieved the package Alma had given her. "I brought supplies to do more cleaning." She glanced down at her muddy shoes and coat. "Myself included!"

"You'll be okay here by yourself?"

"I'll be fine, Grandpa. They're too cowardly to try anything in the daytime. Besides, at twenty-four I can't act like a baby when there's work to do."

"Feed Billy's pigeons, too, will you?"

Ruth nodded and he hurried away.

She turned toward the two-story house, trying to shake off the fear and sadness the incident had brought back. As she remembered the day the Nakamuras were forced from their home, Suzi's parting words echoed in her ears. "Don't worry, Ruth. The Lord will be with us in the camp just as He was with us here. And think of all the people we can tell about Him. He's giving us a mission field." Her faith had shone through the tears in her eyes.

Lord, I wouldn't see opportunity instead of anger, she thought as she approached the farmhouse. *I wish I had Suzi's trust.*

A gust of wind blew scraps of paper across the yard and banged the screen door against the house. She picked up a paper as it tumbled over her feet and stared at the 100% she had marked on Amy Nakamura's math paper. March 23, 1942. She shook her head and ran her finger over the date Amy had written only a month ago. Now, to many people this gentle Christian family had become the enemy.

She stopped at a faucet on the side of the house and washed the mud off her hands. "But there's no hope for my shoes or my coat," she muttered, scraping her muddy shoes on the grass.

"Meow."

She started at the sound, then laughed as a small orange cat bounded out from under the porch to chase a paper blowing by. "You startled me, Fluffy! It's so quiet here I'm getting jumpy." Ruth picked up the cat and walked to the porch steps. Fluffy purred loudly and snuggled against her. "Let's get out of this wind. You're supposed to stay at Grandpa Peterson's while Amy's gone. Why do you keep coming back home?" She scratched Fluffy's ear. "Mice taste better here?"

She slipped off her shoes and coat, then pulled the key from her pocket and reached for the door. Stains of spattered egg and anti-Japanese graffiti were still evident even after all the scrubbing they'd done.

At her touch the door swung open. She hesitated, looking around. "Anyone here?" Only silence answered her. "I'm sure I locked up after we cleaned last time. I hope no one broke in again." She poked her head through the doorway into the kitchen. Her heart skipped a beat. "Doesn't look as if anything's been disturbed, Fluffy." She held the cat closer. "Big help you'd be, but I feel better having something alive with me."

The cozy kitchen was clean and tidy again and waiting for the Nakamuras to gather around the large oak table. Books were back in order on shelves extending along the east wall. And above the stove Suzi's beautifully lettered motto declared the faith the family lived by: "The Lord is my Shepherd."

What a mess this was! she remembered. Eggs had been thrown inside the house, too. Windows broken. Glassware destroyed. Furniture overturned and smashed. Books torn and scattered everywhere. The Ladies Aid had attacked it with mops, brooms, and scrub brushes while Grandpa Peterson and the men worked on the damaged furniture.

Ruth filled a pail with soapy water and carried it to the dining room. "It would be so easy to stay angry," she said aloud, "but Suzi wouldn't want that. 'Look for the Lord's nugget of gold in your troubles,' she'd say. 'He always hides one in there, but remember, if you're angry, you'll miss it.' "

She scraped at a hardened chunk of egg yolk and hummed one of Suzi's favorite songs to counter the anger she felt at the senseless damage. " 'Count your blessings; name them one by one,' " she sang softly as she worked. " 'Count your blessings; see what God has done.' " She stepped back and checked her work. "This war's bringing so many woes right now it's easy to forget the blessings."

She picked up the bucket and carried it to the sink to dump the dirty water. Suddenly she froze as footsteps moved across the porch and the door rattled.

"Yoo-hoo, are you in there, Ruth?" Marge Evans's voice sounded from the porch as she rapped on the kitchen door.

Ruth let out her breath in relief. "I'm in the kitchen, Marge. Come on in," she called out as she rinsed the pail and set it down, her heart still pounding.

Marge stepped into the room, patting her blond windblown hair and pulling her coat back in order. "I declare, Oregon's not a state for women and hairdos!"

Ruth laughed as she wiped her hands and surveyed her friend. "I don't know about that, Marge. Looks like the wind raised your pompadour another inch. You'd never have managed that hairdo on your own," she teased.

"I'll ignore that!" Marge tossed her head and glanced

around the room. "What a difference! I haven't seen it since you ladies cleaned it up." She ran her hand over a chair. "Your grandpa did a great job repairing the furniture, too."

Ruth nodded. "A lot of work, but it's getting there. We want to have it ready when the Nakamuras come back. Hopefully soon."

"Oh, did you hear?" Marge took off her coat and laid it on a chair. "The latest rumor says Leland Hinson and a cousin of his were part of the gang that ransacked this place."

Ruth hung up the towel. "Grandma Peterson says it's hate looking for an excuse to land somewhere."

"It sure landed here. What they wrote on the door was awful!" Marge declared.

Ruth put the cleaning supplies under the sink. "Here on the West Coast people are afraid we'll be bombed or invaded by Japan. And some just want an excuse to hate." She described to Marge the incident she had experienced on her way over. "I don't know the man who stopped to help me, but I'm glad someone was there for me, embarrassing as it was." She wiped the bucket and hung the rag to dry. "Are you going to the community meeting at the school this afternoon? It's about the war effort on the home front."

"That's one reason I stopped by," Marge said. "To see if you were going, I mean. Your grandma said you were over here cleaning and feeding Billy's pigeons."

Ruth leaned against the counter. "Grandpa and I promised Suzi and Nak we'd look after the place for them, and that includes Billy's pigeons. Grandpa took most of the other animals to his place, but it was easier to leave the pigeons here."

Marge put down the package she carried and leaned over a book on the table. "Ruth, look at this. I can't believe they left their Bible behind. They read it all the time." A large Bible lay open in the center of the table.

"They took a small one with them," Ruth explained as she joined Marge at the table. "They always left this one open to the chapter they were reading. Suzi wanted it to stay at the center of their home while they're gone." She peered at the book—Psalm 23. "Be their Shepherd, Lord, and keep them safe wherever they are," she prayed softly.

"Amen to that!" Marge added. She reached into the package. "I brought supplies so we can start repairing the books that were damaged." She took out glue and tape. As she sat down, her toe hit an object that slid out from under the table. "What in the world. . .?"

"Ben-Hur!" Ruth bent to pick up the book. "So that's where it was. Suzi wanted to take it with her, but she couldn't find it." She adjusted Suzi's bookmark and laid the book on the shelf.

"Here you go." Ruth carried a pile of damaged books over to Marge and sat down. "Our local librarian to the rescue." She smiled at her friend and handed her a book. "Your expertise in book repair is greatly appreciated."

"Glad to help. I had to work the day you ladies cleaned." Marge concentrated on the torn spine of the book, then glanced at her friend sideways. "But now let's get to important things—like matters of the heart!" She put the book down and looked at her friend intently. "So, tell me, what's been going on with you and Harold since he went overseas?" she pried. "I've been gone so long; I'm way behind on the life and loves of Ruth Sinclair. Rumor says he was injured in combat. What's happening?"

Ruth pushed a strand of dark brown hair from her face. "I'm not sure, Marge. Pilots stationed overseas are too busy to write these days, I guess. His mother says he's been in the thick of the fighting. His plane was hit and barely made it back to the base. According to her he wasn't badly injured, but I haven't heard from him in ages."

"I don't understand." Marge looked up and frowned. "I know we haven't had time to talk much since I moved back here, but we were best friends, Ruth Sinclair. There's trouble in paradise and you didn't tell me?" Marge pursed her red lips. "You have some explaining to do!"

Ruth's fingers traced the red-and-white-checkered patterns in the oilcloth table covering. "Marge, when Harold and I dated in high school, I was sure we'd get married someday, but we drifted apart in college. Afterwards, when he moved back here and we started dating again. . ."

Ruth sighed. "I thought my dreams were coming true till I found out he was running with a wild crowd. I couldn't believe some of his language or the parties he wanted to go to. And he hardly ever went to church anymore. I tried to talk to him, but. . ." She took a deep breath.

"But trying to save him from himself didn't work, I guess," Marge ventured softly as she reached for a book.

"Once we got back together, I thought he'd be the guy I'd always known." Ruth shook her head. "But, no, it didn't work."

"You should have settled this before he went overseas. You know, talked it out and decided one way or the other," Marge declared firmly.

"I tried, Marge. I told him I couldn't spend my life with someone who didn't have the same values I did. We had a big fight, and then he told me he was leaving to be a pilot for the Royal Air Force in England. He thought of it as a big lark and said this would get the adventurous spirit, as he called it, out of his system. It was so dangerous over there; I didn't have the heart to insist we were through for good."

"I'm confused." Marge frowned as she applied glue to the book spine. "Did you promise to wait for him or what?" She peered up at her friend as glue ran down the book and onto the table. She quickly reached for a rag.

"No, not exactly. Actually, I'm not sure what I promised, Marge. He begged me to write him. He said it would help to have a girl back home when he was in the thick of things." Ruth twisted a strand of hair between her fingers.

"A girl back. . .Ruth! He's just trying to keep you on a string while he lives as he pleases over there. You need to tell him to take that string and go fly a kite instead!" Marge drummed her long red nails on the table.

"Dear John letters are so low, Marge; how could I? There he is risking his life and even getting injured. Besides, maybe the war will wake him up. According to the few letters I've received, so far it hasn't worked at all, but he should be home on leave soon, and we'll settle it then."

Marge laid the book aside and put her hand over Ruth's. "I'm sorry you and Harold ended up like this, Ruth, but it's time for you to move on. Harold has!"

"But, Mar—"

"Ruth, face it. It's over!" Marge patted her hand. "But you're not alone. I'm here, and I'm putting myself in charge of your future!" Marge's eyes twinkled. "What you need is someone new in your life, and I'm the one to help you find him. No one's better at matching up couples than Marge Evans," she declared smugly. "Remember how well I did with Tom and Betty and Mark and Ellen? And Jack and me, of course." The diamond on her finger sparkled in the light.

"Marge, I don't need your help. I'm not looking for anyone right now," Ruth protested. "I have to settle things with Harold first."

"That's why you need me. I'll save you from yourself!" Marge put the repair materials back in the package. "It's a good thing I got this job at the library and moved back here, or who knows what would have happened to you!"

"Marge, I. . ."

"Remember this, Ruth. Harold tied you down here, knowing your sense of loyalty. But if I know the new Harold, he's having a wild time over there while you just sit here. I won't allow it!" Marge shook her finger in Ruth's face.

Ruth grabbed her friend's hand. "I know you mean well, Marge, but I can't. This has to be settled the right way. Dad always taught us to stand by our word no matter what. I have to wait till Harold comes home and settle this face-to-face."

"You can't keep me from trying, Ruth Sinclair. It's for your own good!" Marge raised an eyebrow at her friend. "Hmm, let's see now." She looked Ruth up and down. "Medium height. That's easier to match. Slim, very pretty—that helps." She reached for a piece of Ruth's shoulder-length hair. "All you do is part it on the side and pull it over with a clip. Now if you had a pompadour. . ."

"Marge!" Ruth looked aghast. "I'm not a horse on an auction block!"

Marge calmly ignored her. "And your clothes are too plain. You need some color and fashion zing. Now if. . ." She paused to study her friend.

Ruth finally exploded. "That's quite enough, Marge Evans! I'm not looking for someone, and I don't need to be analyzed!"

"Temper, temper. It's for your own good," Marge insisted, ignoring her protests. "I'm a matchmaking success because I analyze and plan carefully, Ruth Sinclair. You just wait. You'll see." She sat back and thought a moment. "Now let's see. Who's single around here? There's Warren Bowman and Herschel Owens and. . ."

"Herschel Owens! Marge! He's old! He must be at least thirty-five, and he lives with his mother! Besides, he's strange. He always makes me feel uncomfortable. I'm not looking for anyone, and there's no one around here even if I were. That's enough of that!"

"I'm just taking inventory, and I have to be thorough." Unperturbed, Marge glanced at her watch. "Lunchtime. Gotta run. Want to go to the meeting together?" She put her coat on and picked up the package of supplies.

"If you start behaving yourself!" Ruth threw Marge a scowl. "Grandpa's driving over. We can stop to get you on the way. That'll save your hairdo," she teased as she put the books back on the shelf.

Marge wrinkled her nose at her friend, pausing at the door to button her coat. "Thanks. With both my parents working at the shipyards there's never a car available. See ya."

Ruth tidied the room and nudged the cat sleeping on a rug by the door. "Let's go, Fluffy. You can't stay in here."

Outside, she put on her muddy shoes and coat and hurried out back to the pen where Billy Nakamura kept his prized pigeons. Fluffy trotted alongside. As Ruth opened the wire cage and poured grain into the feeder, Fluffy made a leap for the open door, missed, and clung to the edge of the cage.

She grabbed the cat and quickly fastened the latch. "To you they're just ten tasty meals, Fluffy. There had better be ten pigeons here when I come back, or you're in trouble! Come on. Let's go home."

She picked up the cat and started toward the path leading to her grandparents' farm. "We'll go this way. It'll be soggy, but there's no use chancing another run-in with that man."

At the edge of the field Ruth paused to gaze at the world she loved. Fields carved out of the woods. Vine maple and dogwood trees. Wildflowers peeping up in the field. Douglas fir trees towering over everything. It all looked so peaceful. "I never dreamed this could be threatened by war," she murmured, "but I can't deny it. Our country's at war with Japan and Germany, and it affects all our lives."

Fluffy gave a wiggle and leaped to the ground, bounding after a robin hopping across the field in search of a worm. "For you, life's easy, Fluffy. Home is wherever there's a bird or a mouse." The robin flew off safely, and the cat bounded back to her. "My world's all turned around. Mom and Dad have moved to work in the war industry. I'm living with Grandma and Grandpa. Bud's in basic training." She shook her head. "I can't imagine my brother in the navy!"

She picked up the cat. "And then there's Harold. Always ready to go when there's a hint of adventure. He had to head for England to help the Royal Air Force, danger and all." Fluffy snuggled up under her chin, purring loudly. "I do worry about him, Fluffy, but things are so different between us now."

She started through the field. "Lord," she whispered, "the world's falling apart. We need You."

two

A large sign posted on the side of the school gym announced the afternoon's event:

Fir Glen Community Meeting
"The Home Front"
Speaker: Jim Griffin,
Community Coordinator of Civilian Defense

"The whole community must be here," Ruth murmured, peering on tiptoe over the crowd at the door as she and Marge edged their way into the gym behind George and Alma Peterson.

The old building felt comfortably warm from the large woodstove at the side of the room. Chairs and benches were lined up in rows facing the stage. People milled about, warming themselves and chatting in small groups.

"Hey, Miss Sinclair!" A short blond-haired boy dressed in army-style boots, rolled-up jeans, and a khaki shirt bounded toward her, working his yo-yo and looking eager. "Think our class'll get to do some stuff to help win the war?"

"Tim, be careful with that or you'll hit someone," Ruth warned, putting out her hand to stop the yo-yo. "The community coordinator's here to tell us what's planned. I'm sure there'll be some way you kids can help."

"Maybe he'll have so much for us to do we won't have time for English and spelling anymore." Tim raised his eyebrows and looked hopeful.

"No such luck." Ruth laughed and patted his shoulder. "If we're that busy, we'll have to start school earlier."

"Oh, no!" Tim wandered off, groaning at the prospect.

"Take your seats, everyone. We need to get started." Joe Duncan's voice boomed over the buzz of conversations. Ruth led the group to four empty seats. Conversations died and attention shifted to Joe Duncan on the wooden stage at one end of the gym.

"I got this job because I can talk so loud." The audience chuckled and nodded. "Don't have much to say, so I'll turn this meeting over to our community coordinator of civilian defense." Joe's voice boomed through the gym. "You all remember Jim Griffin. Went to school here in Fir Glen. After college, he went off to work in California, and now he's back to help his dad run Griffin's Container Company. Got himself appointed coordinator of this-here civilian defense. Jim, it's yours." He gave a sigh of relief and returned to his seat.

A tall, dark-haired man in the front row stood and walked to the stage. Wind rattled the windows and whined mournfully around the corners of the old gym as the people watched curiously.

"I remember him," Marge leaned over and whispered to Ruth. "He was three grades ahead of us. All the girls thought he was so good-looking. He still is!" She paused. "I didn't realize he'd moved back here." She glanced at Ruth sideways. "Beth Marshall heard he's single. Hmm. . ."

"Shh, let's listen." Ruth scooted in her seat so she could see around the woman in front of her. She looked at the man carefully and nudged her friend. "Marge, that's the man who stopped to help me this morning." Ruth settled back in her seat as the speaker began.

"It's been a while, but I see a lot of familiar faces out there." Jim Griffin smiled and scanned the audience. "When I went to school here, Fir Glen was a community of friendly people always willing to help someone else. I'm counting on that now. The war effort needs the help of all of us, young and old."

"Kids, too?" Tim Henderson piped up, then ducked as his mother leaned over to shush him.

"Yes," Jim nodded seriously, "kids, too. We have a big job

ahead of us." He looked out at the crowd. "I'll be coordinating the defense and war-related efforts for Fir Glen. That includes air-raid drills, blackouts, scrap drives, volunteer projects, rationing—whatever it takes to help the war effort and keep us safe."

He shuffled through the papers he held. "First, I want to introduce volunteers who will fill important posts. Bob Miller will be our air-raid warden. You all know Bob, owner of Fir Glen Market across the road."

Bob jumped to his feet, proudly waving a hand in the air and beaming as the audience applauded. He hooked his thumbs in his suspenders and rocked forward on his toes. "I'm in charge of air-raid drills and the blackout," he announced. "You'll hear from me if there's any light showing from your windows at night. Keep them blackout curtains closed!"

Marge nudged Ruth. "We're in for it now. That authority'll go to his head for sure!"

Ruth smiled and nodded. "He reminds me of Grandpa's bantam roosters—cocky and always strutting around." She watched Bob's suspenders snap back into place as he removed his thumbs.

"Bob's also volunteered the lot behind his store for our scrap drives, starting with tires and any rubber we can scavenge," Jim continued. He looked at his papers. "Next volunteer is Joe Duncan." Joe bobbed up and down, ducking his head shyly at the applause. "Here on the West Coast we have to be prepared for a Japanese attack at any time," Jim declared seriously.

A murmur ran through the crowd. People looked at each other, fear reflecting on their faces.

"Joe will head up the Ground Observer Corps. Any comments, Joe?"

"We need volunteers. See me after the meeting to sign up," Joe called out. "You'll be trained to identify any enemy aircraft you see and phone in the information. The observer post will be set up on the feed store roof. We need to keep that post manned!"

"And," Jim added, "scrap paper can be dropped off at the feed store. You kids will have a lot of collecting to do." He looked over at Tim, who grinned at his classmates and waved at Ruth.

Jim paused and looked out at the crowd. "Now to the part you've been reading about in the *Oregonian*. We'll have to make sacrifices to win this war. That includes rationing. Tires were rationed back in January. The next item will be sugar."

"Oh, no!" A groan broke out spontaneously from the younger generation scattered throughout the room.

Jim continued. "On May 4 through 7, you'll register here at the school so every individual can receive a sugar book, as we call it. One person from your family can register for the entire household. Each month you'll be allowed about two pounds of sugar per person."

A lady in the third row stood. "Most of us bake and can our own fruit. How will we get by?" She sat down to a murmur of agreement throughout the audience.

"This threatens my sweet tooth, too," Jim admitted, "but I know you'll all join me in making any sacrifice to win this war." He smiled and patted his waistline. "And think how slim and trim we'll be without all those desserts!"

The crowd chuckled and nodded.

"When you go to the market, you'll turn in stamps from your ration book in order to buy sugar," he continued and held up a sample booklet. "No stamps, no sugar. And," he warned, "the stamps must be torn out of the book in the presence of the store clerk, or they become void."

He paused and looked around at the crowd. "To prevent hoarding, the stamps are coded so they're good for about a month. After that they'll expire. In order to get the next ration book, you'll be required to turn in the old one, so don't throw the book away when it's empty or expired."

People in the audience glanced about uncertainly as Jim explained the regulations.

"And be sure to check your sugar supply before you come

so you can tell us how much you have on hand," he added. He looked over at Tim and his friends. "Since we'll register all day on May 4, the school board has canceled classes for the day."

A buzz of excitement ran through the children till frowns from their parents silenced them.

Jim added, "The rest of the week you can register after school."

Ruth watched the speaker. *Marge's right,* she thought. *He is good-looking. Dark hair. Maybe six foot. Friendly, with an easy confidence.* She heard him mention teachers, and her thoughts turned back to the speech.

"Our dedicated teachers," Jim was saying, "will be in charge of the registration, with help from our local women's club. Could we have the teachers stand, please?" Ruth blushed and rose to her feet along with three other women.

"Ah, yes, Mrs. Foster. Our favorite first- and second-grade teacher." Mrs. Foster nodded to the group and smiled.

Jim continued. "Mrs. Christianson. It's been a long time. For you, probably not long enough. As I recall, I wiggled my way through third and fourth grades."

Mrs. Christianson laughed and protested. "But you were still a good student, Jim."

"And Mrs. Hastings. By the time I was in your seventh- and eighth-grade room, we had become a little too well acquainted in your principal's office, I'm afraid." As the audience chuckled, he turned to Ruth. "And this is. . ."

"That's Miss Sinclair," Tim announced. "She's my teacher."

Jim smiled at her and paused.

He recognizes me, Ruth thought. *He wouldn't dare explain in front of everyone!* She shifted uncomfortably, and the room suddenly felt extremely warm.

"I know I wasn't in your class. Glad to meet you, Miss Sinclair." Jim smiled at her as she blushed again and grate-fully sat down with the other teachers. "I'll meet with you ladies this week to brief you on the registration procedures. Is

Tuesday after school okay?" His glance rested on Ruth while the other teachers nodded their approval.

"Now let me call your attention to the posters." Jim pointed to the array on the gym wall. "You'll see these all over. They're to remind you and inspire you." On one Uncle Sam pointed and declared, "I want you," while another promoted war bonds.

Arlan Anderson stood up. "With so many people working at Swan Island Shipyards, we need to pay special attention to these." He pointed to a cluster of posters: "Loose talk kills." "A slip of the lip may sink a ship." "Don't tell secrets." "You never know who might be a spy these days, so be careful what you say!"

"Good point, Arlan; one we need to take seriously," Jim commented. "I guess that's it for now. We'll post announcements at Bob's market and the feed store. Check their bulletin boards often." He paused and looked out at the audience. His eye caught Ruth's for a moment, and he smiled.

"One more thing. I think I should say this straight out and get it over with. Many of you have a brother, uncle, son, or husband in the service." Heads nodded here and there. "I'm doing all I can here because the service wouldn't take me. Too many ear infections as a child, and I ended up with a broken eardrum. But I promise to work hard on this end to keep us safe. Now let's have Pastor Cameron lead us in prayer for our country, and then we'll close with 'God Bless Our Native Land.'"

As the singing faded and people rose to leave, a small figure pushed through the crowd. "Hey, Miss Sinclair, I'm gonna collect papers and catch some spies! Me and Charlie are starting a detective club!" Tim bounded up, looking thrilled.

George chuckled. "What are you going to do? Knock 'em out with your yo-yo?"

"Hey, good idea, Mr. Peterson!" Tim grinned and wandered away with his friends, whispering plans for detecting spies.

Alma chatted with neighbors as they worked their way to

the door. George followed patiently behind his wife.

"He noticed you," Marge whispered to Ruth. "Did you see it? Jim Griffin kept looking right at you. He's interested in you." She spoke excitedly. "You need someone new in your life, and he'll be perfect."

"Marge!" Ruth ignored her and peered ahead to see what was slowing their exit. By the door she saw Jim Griffin meeting the people as they left the building. She felt a nervous flutter. As they approached the door, Marge nudged her. She scowled back.

Jim held out his hand and grasped hers warmly. "Ah, the new teacher. I'm glad to meet you—again." He smiled and continued to hold her hand.

Ruth smiled back. "Thank you again for your help, Mr. Griffin." She pulled her hand away and moved on.

As they stepped outside, Marge gushed, "He's even better looking up close. How can he still be single?" She muttered under her breath, "Jack, Jack, Jack," and winked at Ruth. "Just reminding myself. If there were to be a temptation, that would be it. But I do love Jack, so I'll leave Mr. Griffin to you."

"Enough of you, Miss Matchmaker. You know the situation. It's not right."

"You two ready?" George interrupted as the wind tore at his hat. "The car's this way."

"If we can tear Ruth away," Marge teased.

"In the car with you." Ruth opened the door for her friend. As she waited for Marge to get in, she glanced toward the building where Jim was greeting the last of the crowd. He was shaking old Mrs. Benson's hand and patting her shoulder.

"And you said there was no one around to get interested in," Marge said smugly as Ruth climbed in and shut the door. "Once I'm on the job, look what turns up. What did I tell you? Matchmaking's a gift I have!"

three

The bell of the white country church resounded throughout the community the next morning, each bong echoing an invitation to come. Ruth stepped into the church entry, clutching her Bible and pulling on her white gloves. She straightened her hat, feeling all askew after an hour in the basement with her fifth- and sixth-grade Sunday school class.

People stood around chatting in small groups as they waited for the service to begin. Spying her grandmother's flowered dress and small black hat, Ruth walked over to the cluster of ladies gathered around Alma Peterson. "We'll meet here in the basement on Tuesday mornings," Alma was saying. "Bring your scrap material and supplies."

She turned as Ruth walked up. "There you are, dear. The Ladies Aid is going to make quilts for English refugees bombed out by the Nazis. Those poor people need anything we can send them. They've lost everything."

"When school's out, you'll have to join us," Hazel Ellison added with a giggle.

Ruth smiled to herself. A better-hearted woman couldn't be found, but she was unique. Whatever Hazel said was accompanied by that giggle. And her hats! A pile of flowers swayed atop the hat as Hazel giggled.

"Ten o'clock Tuesday morning, ladies," Alma reminded them and took Ruth's elbow. "Grandpa's saving us a seat. We'd better sit before people think we're the choir marching in. Wouldn't they be sorry!" Alma bustled away to join her husband.

As the congregation sang the opening hymn, Ruth looked around the sanctuary. The old pews were worn by worshippers who had come faithfully over the years to praise God and

26

pray. Again they came on this morning to beseech God's help for their country and to thank Him for His blessings. She studied the people. With the world at war, what would happen to their lives? What sacrifices would they be called on to make? Her mind drifted to people in the war zones and the extreme sacrifices they were facing.

She was drawn back to the service as Pastor Cameron stepped to the pulpit and looked out at his congregation. "My friends," he began, "we live in fearful times. Each day's news is worse than that of the day before. The Japanese have taken Guam, Manila, and places most of us had never heard of before the war. We read of horrors like Bataan and its death march."

A child dropped a hymnal, and the congregation jumped.

"Fear grips our land," he continued. "A cruel and inhuman evil strides through the world. Is Satan winning? Will he be victorious?"

The congregation grew quieter. Even the children were still. Ruth glanced around at the people she had known since she was a child spending summers at her grandparents' farm. Good people. Not perfect but good-hearted and hardworking. As her eyes moved down the rows, she saw Jim Griffin sitting with his parents, intent on the pastor's words.

"In the months ahead you'll be hearing about V for victory." The pastor held up his hand in the victory sign. "Victory gardens. Victory homes. We must all do our part to stop this evil and defend our human freedom, but can man by himself defeat evil?"

Ruth could see heads firmly shaking.

"Never!" the pastor continued. "Our men in the service are paying a price to contain evil, but they cannot defeat it forever. Only God can do that. He, too, had to pay a price—the life of Christ, His only Son. On the cross Christ defeated death, Satan, and evil with His life."

Heads of the congregation members nodded their agreement. Ruth could see Hazel Ellison's flowers bobbing.

"V for victory? Yes, but for us it's C for victory—Christ's

victory. We must all do our parts, but our main battle must be on our knees in prayer."

Ruth glanced over at Jim. His face was serious and his head nodded in agreement.

"So I implore you to join in the war effort every way you can, but I implore you above all else to pray without ceasing. Remember, the only true victory is in Christ. Amen." He shut his Bible. "Let's close with 'Onward Christian Soldiers.' "

As the hymn faded, the congregation rose. "He sure got to the bottom of it," George Peterson commented as they left the pew. "If people hadn't left God out of things, we wouldn't be in this mess."

"Prayer is the only way," Alma agreed.

As Ruth followed her grandparents, a deep voice sounded to her left. "Hello again. Miss Sinclair, isn't it?"

She turned to see Jim Griffin smiling at her. "Yes, I'm the teacher you didn't have," she replied and smiled. "The one who takes mud baths in public."

Jim chuckled. "My loss, though I am glad to meet you now instead of as a student. As for the mud baths, you're a living ad for their effectiveness. Say. . ."

"Hey, Miss Sinclair!" Tim Henderson pushed his way through the crowd and shook her arm. "Mr. Griffin's gonna coach our youth softball team. I'm gonna play first base! C'mon, Mr. Griffin. The guys are waiting for you. We need to plan our first practice." He tugged at Jim's sleeve. "C'mon, Mr. Griffin."

"I guess I'm needed for critical defense planning. I'll see you Tuesday at the meeting, Miss Sinclair." He winked at her as Tim led him away.

Ruth took a deep breath and followed her grandparents out of the church.

"He's a nice young man," Alma commented. "And he's in church on Sunday, too." Ruth knew her grandmother's comment referred to Harold's infrequent attendance.

Outside, worshippers hurried to their cars in the blustery

April wind. Ruth and her grandparents escaped to their car as a gust swirled around them. "I got the repairs done on Suzi's lamp table," George said as he pulled out of the church parking lot. "I'd like to drop it off at the Nakamuras' on the way home. Do you have the key with you, Ruth?"

She fished around in her purse. "It's right here, Grandpa. I keep it with me."

George nodded and turned toward the Nakamura farm.

As they pulled into the driveway, Ruth again felt the emptiness of the place that had been so full of life such a short time ago. Sunday dinners had been great times here, discussing the sermon and talking about the season's garden or new crochet patterns. Afterwards, Suzi loved to adjourn to the living room for a session of gospel songs around the piano.

"Don't be long. I have a roast in the oven," Alma warned as George parked by the back porch.

"Here, I'll help you, Grandpa." Ruth jumped out and held the trunk lid as George removed the small table. "Let me get the door open." She hurried up the porch steps as a gust tugged at her coat.

They stepped out of the wind into the tidy kitchen. "I'll put this where it belongs and be right back," George said as he carried the table to the living room.

Ruth walked to the kitchen table and stared. "How did this get here?" She frowned at Suzi's copy of *Ben-Hur* lying on the table. "I thought I put it back on the shelf yesterday."

She glanced around the room. The door had been locked and the windows repaired or boarded over. Everything seemed to be in order. She took a deep breath. "Where's your common sense, Ruth Sinclair?" she chided herself "Books don't hop around a room, and the house was locked up, so no one could get in."

She paused and felt goose bumps on her arms. "Could someone else have a key? No, that can't be. I have the only one. Either I'm getting old and forgetful, or Marge left it there and I didn't notice."

She shook off the uncomfortable sensation and picked up the book. "Suzi promised I could read it after her. She'd be happy to know I'm taking care of it while she's gone." She tucked it under her arm.

"Talking to yourself again, Ruth?" George teased as he appeared in the doorway. He glanced around the room and nodded in approval. "Looks mighty good after the ladies tackled the mess." He shook his white head. "Sure too bad what those hoodlums did. Well, let's go home to dinner. I'm ready for Grandma's roast!"

❧

Ruth looked up from *Ben-Hur* to find the afternoon's light fading. George was finishing his chores while Alma crocheted a doily for the center of the dining room table. The old country home George and Alma had built forty years earlier was warm and cozy. A fire crackled in the fireplace, adding a homey touch as well as its warmth. The wallpaper was faded and old-fashioned, but to Ruth it meant something in the world stayed the same.

"Time to close the blackout curtains, Grandma, or Bob Miller will be after us." Ruth got up and wrinkled her nose. "Such a cheery color." She pulled the opaque black curtains closed, making sure no light escaped around the edges.

Alma chuckled. "Bob does get carried away, but he's right. We don't want our lights to make us targets for Japanese bombers."

Ruth picked up *Ben-Hur* and looked around for Suzi's bookmark. Not finding it, she absently reached for a piece of paper to mark her place. "I wonder where Bud'll be stationed, Grandma. The censors cut so much out of his letters sometimes that you can't tell what he's saying." She held the book tightly. "I hope he isn't assigned to one of the battleships in the Pacific. That's so dangerous."

Alma nodded. "And that reminds me. I need to get material to make a banner for our window to show someone from our family's in the service. We're proud Bud's serving his country."

She reached for a piece of paper and a pencil. "Let's see. It takes blue for the star, white satin for the background, and red felt for the border." She busied herself determining the material she'd need.

Ruth got up with a loud sigh. "I'm going upstairs to correct some papers, Gram."

Alma looked up from her calculations. "You sound sad and lonely tonight, dear. This war's brought so many changes to our world. Adjusting takes time."

"I know, Grandma, but I miss everyone the most on Sundays—Bud, my folks, the Nakamuras. Remember the wonderful Sunday afternoons we had together?"

Alma patted her arm. "I remember, dear. They were good days."

Ruth hugged Alma and touched her cheek gently. "I love you, Gram."

Upstairs, she plopped down on her tall feather bed and looked around. "This was Mom's old room. I wonder if she sat here dreaming and trying to understand life, too." Ruth looked at the pink-flowered wallpaper and the dark dresser with its oval mirror. She imagined her mother sitting there primping for a date with her father. Her mother patted her hair, then skipped down the stairs to greet her date. Her father looked handsome and smiled at her as she took his arm. Ruth sighed.

She pulled her knees up to her chest and rested her chin on them. "Why do I feel so lonely on Sundays?" she asked aloud. She sat up and reached for the math papers she needed to correct. "I guess because Sunday is a family day, and that's all changed now. I told Marge I wasn't looking for anyone. It's true, but I guess I'm missing someone—and I'm not sure who it is."

She turned back to the papers, but again her mind wandered, and she pictured herself peering through the living room window at her parents as they left on their date. They smiled into each other's eyes, unaware of anyone else in the world.

With a sigh she put the papers aside and reached for her journal. She opened it and stared at the blank page as she nibbled on the end of her pencil. Slowly, words flowed onto the page. She took a deep breath and sat back to read.

Love*
It came and it went
Like the time that I spent
In my dreams that were all about you.

Time came and time left
Like the hope that I let
Fill my heart and my soul about you.

Love came and love's gone
Like the words in a song
That I listened to thinking about you.

It came and it went
Like the time that I've spent
In these words that I've written about you.

She put the journal down and ran her hand over the cover. *Time and love are slipping away,* she thought, *and I can't seem to grasp either one anymore.*

---

*poem by Kelly Croston Kalthoff, 1989.

four

"Class dismissed!" The words were barely out of Ruth's mouth before the children hurried to the door.

"Hey, Miss Sinclair, I'm gonna go collect newspapers. Then me and Charlie are gonna look for spies." Tim raced for the door.

"It's Charlie and I, Tim. Don't forget your spelling book. There's a test tomorrow," Ruth reminded him.

Grumbling, he returned to his desk.

"So this is the fifth- and sixth-grade room," Jim Griffin spoke from the doorway. "It hasn't changed much since I spent two years in here." He looked at the penmanship examples along the front blackboard and the pictures of presidents on the side wall. The desks were in straight rows, one attached to another.

"You went to school here, Mr. Griffin? Wow, I didn't know the school was that old! Well, see ya." Tim ran from the room, his spelling book under his arm.

"How's that for a quick aging?" Jim grinned. "Just call me old man Griffin."

Ruth laughed. "The kids think we're fossils." She picked up her notebook. "The meeting's in Mrs. Hastings's room. Shall we go?"

"Ladies," Jim began as he addressed the four teachers, "these are the forms to be filled out so each family can receive its ration books. Take a look at them, and we'll discuss your questions."

The teachers read over the forms, and Jim explained the regulations. As the discussion wound down, he pushed back his chair. "Remember—it's very important to note how much sugar they have at home. They'll be allowed a small amount

33

without losing any stamps from their sugar books. Now, if there are no more questions, I'll be here with the materials bright and early Tuesday morning."

He gathered his papers together. "Oh, one more thing. The government doesn't provide any help for the community coordinator, so I'm looking for a volunteer assistant. I thought one of you would be a good choice. Anyone volunteer?"

Mrs. Foster spoke up quickly. "Three of us are busy with families. I think Miss Sinclair would be the logical one. Don't you ladies agree?" She looked around at the other teachers, who nodded their approval.

"Good idea," Jim interjected quickly. "That's four votes yes. Miss Sinclair it is." He looked at Ruth. "You do volunteer, don't you?"

"A rather heavy-handed approach, I must say," Ruth replied good-naturedly, "but, yes, I'll do it. I've wanted to get more involved in the war effort, and this could be a good way."

"Great." Jim collected his papers. "I'm late for an appointment. I'll get in touch with you later in the week about your job." He grabbed his briefcase. "It will be a pleasure working with you, Miss Sinclair." With a wink he hurried from the room.

&

"Red light, green light!" a child called out as Ruth watched the children enjoy their recess on a sunny spring morning. The air was clear and fresh, and a robin warbled from a nearby tree.

"Do they still play king of the mountain and Mother, may I?"

Ruth turned to see Jim Griffin standing with his hands in his pockets, enjoying the children's play.

"I loved this old school at recess. The trees and the creek ditch were great places for hide-and-seek," he reminisced.

"Yes, and they still play tag, jump rope, and softball. Oh, and red rover, red rover. . ."

"Send someone right over," Jim finished and laughed as shouts sounded from the ball field.

"Tag him, tag him!"

"He's out!"

"No, he's not!" Voices rose in argument, then play resumed.

"Those were good days," Ruth agreed.

Jim looked over at her. "I stopped by to see if we can get together after school to discuss the work you'll do. How about meeting at Sandy's Café for an ice-cream soda to inspire us as we talk? At, say, 3:30?"

Ruth nodded. "That's fine with me. Oh, there's the bell. Recess is over. See you at Sandy's." She smiled and turned toward the building. Jim gave a wave of his hand as he walked away.

❧

At 3:30 Ruth entered the café and sat down in a red-and-chrome booth by the window. An array of war-related posters covered the walls. "Uncle Sam wants you" seemed to point right at her.

"I'll never smile again until I smile at you," Frank Sinatra crooned from the jukebox. Memories flooded over her. All those times she and Harold had met in this café. She could picture him sitting across from her, his blond head tilted in that special way as he smiled at her. It seemed so long ago.

If he hadn't changed, what would my life be now? she wondered. But he had.

She shook her head to clear out the memories and picked up *Ben-Hur. Jim's late,* she thought, *but that's never a waste for a bookworm.* She found her place and tried to read, but her mind wandered. *When Harold's so far away, it's easy to forget how much he changed. And I do miss the way he used to be. What will he be like when he comes home? Will the war wake him up?*

When she looked up, she saw a man staring at her intently. He seemed vaguely familiar. Who. . .? The man in the old car! The one who had shouted at her the day she fell on Suzi's driveway. Why would he be so interested in her? She moved uncomfortably, then looked up quickly as a voice sounded beside her.

"Hi. Sorry I'm late. We had a problem at the plant." Jim smiled warmly at her as he stopped beside the booth and took off his overcoat. "I'll get the sodas and be right back. What kind would you like?"

"Strawberry's fine," she replied. As Jim turned to get their order, she looked toward the man at the counter. He was slumped over a cup of coffee. She studied him carefully, remembering the words he had shouted at her.

"Best fifteen-cent sodas around." Jim returned and set two ice-cream sodas on the table. "Now, first things first." He settled into the booth. "I never work with someone I don't know, so tell me about Miss Sinclair. I'd prefer to call you Ruth, if you don't mind."

"No, that's fine," Ruth replied and took a sip of her soda. "There's not much to tell. I went to the teacher's college down in Monmouth. My dad's an engineer, so my folks moved to help set up the war industry. With housing so tight, it wasn't fair for me to take up a whole house. They leased it out, and I moved out to Grandma and Grandpa's farm. And you?"

"University of Oregon. Business major. I always planned to take over for Dad at the factory." Jim peered around her soda. "I don't see a ring on that finger. Unattached?"

Ruth twirled the soda glass back and forth in her hands. "I've been dating Harold Ramsdale on and off for several years. He's a pilot with the Royal Air Force."

Jim raised his eyebrows. "Any commitment?"

She shifted in her seat. "Harold has to get his fill of adventure before he settles down, but he thinks. . ." She hesitated. "I promised to write," she finished lamely. She looked down at the soda. *It's true,* she thought, *but why didn't I explain?*

Jim smiled. "That's encouraging. You're not taken then. So how about joining me for dinner?"

She took a deep breath. "I can't, Jim. Harold and I are still together—sort of. For me there are some big problems, but he's over there risking his life. It wouldn't be right." She was surprised to feel a stab of disappointment.

Jim was quiet a moment. He looked at her and nodded. "I understand. Actually, I admire loyalty, especially to someone over there, fighting, while I have to sit home." He smiled. "So, friends?"

Ruth nodded.

"Friends—unless there's a change in your status?" He cocked an eyebrow hopefully.

"You're an impossible flirt, Mr. Griffin."

"This doesn't mean it's back to Mr. Griffin."

"Okay, Jim."

He reached for his briefcase. "Now, about the job. We can't talk much here." He pointed toward a poster that warned the enemy is listening. "Right now I need someone to do paperwork for me—file, type, post notices—that kind of thing. How does that sound?"

"I'm not the world's best secretary, but I can handle that. When do I start?"

"Anytime this weekend. I need these notices typed and posted at Fir Glen Market and Joe's Feed Store." He handed her several pages.

"No problem." She put the papers with her book. "Jim, do you know that man at the counter, dark-haired with a beard, slumped over his coffee?"

Jim turned around. "I've never seen him before. Why?"

"He was the one who shouted at me the day you helped me out of the mud. He keeps staring at me."

"Maybe he has good taste in women but bad manners," Jim teased.

"No, seriously, Jim, he's very anti-Japanese. He let me know in no uncertain terms what he thought of their friends, too."

"Let me know if he gives you any problems." Jim rose from the booth. "Since you won't go to dinner with me, I'll let you go home and write your letters. Isn't that what girls back home do on Friday nights?" He opened the door, and they walked out.

"Well, well, out on the town, I see." Marge walked up, smiling smugly.

Ruth turned to greet her friend. "And what are you doing out of your library, Marge Evans?"

"Meeting Beth Marshall for a Coke." She looked at Jim. "Don't I get a personal introduction, Ruth, or are you trying to keep him all to yourself?" A mischievous smile played at her mouth.

Ruth shifted the papers she carried and made the introduction, giving Marge a sideways scowl.

Jim reached out his hand. "Glad to meet you, Marge Evans." He raised his eyebrows. "So this is where the good-looking women of Fir Glen congregate."

Marge grinned. "Umm, Ruth, you didn't tell me he was so charming, too." She glanced at the frown on Ruth's red face, enjoying her friend's discomfort.

Ruth changed the subject. "I can't stay and chat, you two. Grandma's waiting for me at the church. Call me, Marge." She thanked Jim for the soda. "I'll get these typed and posted right away."

She hurried to her car. As she took out her keys, the papers she held slid to the ground. She quickly bent to retrieve them as the wind scattered them under the car next to hers. Crouched between the vehicles, she could hear Marge's voice from the distance.

"Good to meet you, Jim. I'd better let you hurry home to get ready for your Friday night date."

Jim sounded sheepish. "I just got turned down. My luck to meet a girl with a guy overseas."

Ruth froze where she was. *Oh, no, Marge, don't you dare!* She could hear her friend pause.

"You mean Ruth?" Marge laughed. "It's not the way she makes it sound, Jim. Her heart's not tied to Harold anymore, just her ethics. She won't write the cad a Dear John letter. She insists on waiting till he comes home to break up."

"I thought they. . ."

A car started near Ruth, drowning out Jim's words.

". . .But he changed. . .played on her sympathies. . ." Snippets of conversation drifted over to her. When the car pulled away, Marge had headed for the café, and Jim was getting in his car.

She held the papers tightly. "I know what you're trying to do, Marge Evans," she murmured, "but it won't work." She got in the car. "I've got to do what I've got to do, whether you understand it or not!"

five

"That's all the sugar we have on hand, dear," Alma called from the pantry as she estimated the number of pounds and put the containers back on the shelf.

Ruth jotted down the information. "I hope everyone remembers to estimate their sugar supply before the rationing registration tomorrow," she commented as she closed her notebook.

"It'll be a challenge to cook with less sugar, but we'll be healthier for it." Alma came into the room, wiping her hands on her apron.

Ruth watched her and smiled. *Except for church, Grandma always wears a full, wraparound apron. It's her uniform— and her hand towel,* she noted fondly. *And I've never seen her do anything slowly.* Alma bustled about the kitchen, clanking the dishes in her haste. Ruth glanced at a cup on the table with a nick in the rim, another result of Alma's fast pace.

❧

The next morning Ruth arrived at the school gym to find Mrs. Hastings taping signs on the tables while Mrs. Foster tacked a poster over the entrance that read: "Sugar Rationing Registration Here."

"Good morning, ladies," Jim Griffin called out as he entered the gym carrying a large box. "Here you are. Straight from the county clerk's office." He set the box down and began to unload registration forms, sugar books, and pencils. "Are you ready?"

"If we can get the children to add and spell, we can register the adults, Jim," Mrs. Hastings responded firmly as she distributed the supplies to the registration tables and assigned each teacher her place.

"Is this where we register?" A man and woman stood in the doorway, looking around uncertainly.

"It sure is. Come on in." Jim greeted the couple and ushered them to a registration table. He turned to the teachers. "I'll leave you ladies to your duties. My dad's a stickler about getting to work on time. I'll drop by at noon to see how you're doing."

Ruth sat down at one of the tables as a small elderly woman approached her.

"Is this where I sign up for our ration books? We have three pounds of sugar at home. That's all." The woman stopped in front of her and smiled. Her well-worn gray coat hung loosely, and a small black hat perched on her head.

"Yes, ma'am. And this is the information we need." Ruth smiled warmly as she laid two forms in front of the woman and started to explain them.

"Oh, no, I can't. I can't do that. I can't read, you see, and I don't write." She clutched her purse in both hands and stood in front of Ruth, waiting.

Ruth picked up the forms. "I'll fill them in for you. Just give me the information and we'll do fine." She smiled at the woman kindly and bent over the forms, asking the required questions. "So far, so good. Now, we need to know your husband's height, ma'am."

"He's about that much taller than I am." The woman spread out her arms and smiled at Ruth.

Ruth stared at her. "How much is that in feet and inches, Mrs. Albers?"

The woman stared back. "You're the teacher, dear. You'll have to figure that out." She smiled and waited.

The briefing hadn't told her what to do in situations like this. Ruth squirmed in her chair.

Mrs. Foster leaned over from her end of the table. "I know them, Ruth. Mr. Albers is about five feet ten inches."

Ruth smiled her gratitude and continued with the form. "We're done, Mrs. Albers. Remember, you can't buy sugar without the ration stamps. Do you understand?" She handed the woman two sugar books.

"Oh, yes, dear. Thank you." Mrs. Albers smiled as she walked away, looking through the ration book.

Ruth glanced over at Mrs. Foster and shook her head. "Would you believe that!"

"Mrs. Albers had very little schooling. She was the second of thirteen children and had to stay home to help her mother," Mrs. Foster explained, then turned to help the couple approaching her table.

A steady flow of people came through the gym all morning. "We'll go to lunch in shifts so someone will be on duty at all times," Mrs. Hastings announced. "Mrs. Christianson and Miss Sinclair may go after they finish their next people. And, remember, the Women's Club will be here to relieve you at three."

Ruth turned to a man in bib overalls standing before her. She smiled. "Good morning, sir. How many people are there in your household?"

"Two, ma'am, but I need three sugar books," the old farmer stated firmly.

"You only get one book per person, sir," Ruth explained as she laid two forms on the table.

"I need three," he repeated. "Need a sugar book for Josephine, too." He stood with his hands in his overall pockets.

Ruth looked puzzled. "Is Josephine a daughter who lives with you?"

The old man chuckled and slapped his leg. "Josephine's my daughter! That's a good one!" He chuckled again. "I need one for Josephine, too. She's not my kin."

"Is she someone who lives as part of your family? You can't register for other than your own household," Ruth repeated patiently.

He chuckled again. "Josephine's my mule."

Ruth's mouth fell open. "Your mule? You want to register your mule?"

He nodded seriously. "She don't do no work unless I give her sugar. Got to keep her going to get the farmwork done. I need a sugar book for Josephine."

"But, sir, I can't do that." *What do I do now?* Ruth thought. *He's dead serious and not budging.* Out of the corner of her eye, she saw Jim Griffin enter the gym and beckoned him over to her table.

"Sir, Mr. Griffin is our community coordinator. He'll explain this to you." She turned to Jim and smiled sweetly. "A problem for the expert." She quickly straightened her table and said to Mrs. Foster, "I'll be in my classroom if you need me." As she hurried away, she could hear Jim trying to convince the farmer that Josephine didn't qualify.

Jim entered her classroom a few minutes later. "A mighty quick exit there, Miss Sinclair. Thanks for leaving him to me. Stubborn as a mule he was. I wasn't sure which was Josephine!"

"Give me a classroom of kids any day!" Ruth replied. "You can't believe the stories people came up with or the problems they had with the form."

Jim sat down at one of the desks. "After that episode I can imagine."

"There was the lady who claimed she had a drawer full of sugar. She had no idea how many pounds were in it or its size. And then there was the one who had about six sugar bowls full." Ruth shook her head.

"Many of these people didn't have much formal education. I run into this all the time at the plant."

Ruth unpacked the lunch her grandmother had prepared and laid it out on her large oak desk. "Join me? Grandma insists on packing my lunch so I'll eat right and sends enough for a farmhand. I'll get fat if I eat all this."

Jim cocked an eyebrow at her. "I can't have you ruining that perfect figure, now can I? I'm honor bound to help out." He reached for a piece of fried chicken and sat back in the seat.

The classroom clock ticked steadily on the wall above the blackboard. Across the room a wall of long, narrow windows gave light to the room. Jim touched an ink bottle set in the small well in the desk and ran his finger over a name carved in the desktop. "If I look I might find my name carved on one of these desks, too." He grinned sheepishly. "I spent some time in Mrs. Hastings's office for that bit of mischief!"

"Jim, I'm shocked! I expected you to be well behaved!" Ruth exclaimed.

"I wasn't really bad, just mischievous—till my dad got ahold of me, that is!" He chuckled as he got up to put the chicken bone in the wastebasket. "These wooden seats were mighty hard sitting for a while after he got through with me!" He glanced at the clock. "Gotta run. Thanks for the lunch." With a wink he left the room.

Ruth returned to the gym, where people arrived in spurts throughout the afternoon. As she waited for the next person, Ruth heard a voice to her right. "Miss Sinclair, had I realized you were on duty I would've registered with you." Ruth looked up to see the large figure of Herschel Owens smiling broadly.

Oh, no, she thought. "Mr. Owens," she answered briefly but politely.

He was looking at his sugar book. "No sacrifice for the war is too much, Miss Sinclair. We must give our best for our country, don't you think?"

A lady stepped up to the table and waited impatiently for Ruth to help her. "I must get back to my duties, Mr. Owens." She turned to the woman in relief as Herschel ambled away. *Marge better not be trying to set me up with him!* she fumed to herself.

"Finally!" Mrs. Foster sighed. "Relief's here. The Women's Club just arrived." She reached out to tidy her table.

Ruth gathered her belongings and hurried from the gym. As she rounded the corner of the building, a green Plymouth drove by. Jim gave a honk and waved. She felt an odd flutter as she smiled and waved back.

The power of suggestion, she thought. *Marge's suggestion. Just ignore it, Ruth,* she told herself and hurried home.

≈

"How'd the registration go?" George Peterson looked up from

his newspaper that evening. He was comfortably settled in his favorite deep blue, overstuffed chair.

"You wouldn't believe it," Ruth said. She sat down and related incidents from the day.

"That will seem easy compared to the gas rationing registration in a few weeks. People won't like having their driving restricted." He put the paper down. "How about a game of checkers, Ruth?"

She saw the gleam in his eye. "Think you're going to beat me again, Grandpa? Not this time." She got out the board and set up her side, enjoying the warm atmosphere of her grandparents' living room.

"Do you have plans for the summer, dear?" Alma asked as she knitted socks for the men overseas.

"Helping you with the garden. Keeping up the Nakamuras' place. And I'll be busy helping Jim Griffin, I'm sure."

"He's such a nice young man. Goes to church every Sunday. Works so hard to help out. He's the settled-down kind." Alma's knitting needles clicked.

"Your move." George sat back smugly.

Ruth looked over the board. "Oh, Grandpa, you did it again. I'm trapped. If I didn't know better, I'd think you conspired with Grandma to divert my attention. Okay, you win again."

"Concentration. That's the key." George got up. "Got to check on the calf."

"How's your work with Mr. Griffin going?" Alma asked. She looked up at Ruth.

"There's not much to do so far—typing mainly. When school's out I'm sure there'll be more."

"No word from Harold?"

"None." Ruth could sense the direction of the conversation.

"Harold's a nice enough man, but I wonder about his faith, dear." Alma stopped her knitting. "Fun and success seem more important to him than the things of the Lord. You need to think about that if you're going to spend your life with someone."

Alma laid her knitting aside and leaned forward. "Could I

ask you something personal, Ruth? Were you really serious about Harold? He didn't seem very settled."

Ruth's fingers played with strands of hair as she paused. "Harold was a lot of fun, Grandma," she answered evasively. "Maybe the war will make him take life more seriously."

"Fun isn't the basis for a solid marriage, Ruth. If God isn't the foundation of your life together, you won't survive the hard times. And, believe me, they'll come."

Ruth sat quietly. "I know you're right, Grandma."

"Tell me about this Mr. Griffin. I think he's interested in you." Alma peered over her wire-frame glasses.

She blushed. "We're just friends. Even if I am rethinking my relationship with Harold, I won't let someone down who's risking his life for his country." She looked at her grandmother. "Jim's a great guy. If there were no obligation to Harold, who knows? But there is. I have to see that through first."

"Talk to the Lord about it, Ruth. He doesn't want you making a mistake. Read Psalm 127. The Lord knows what's best for us." Her knitting needles clicked rapidly.

"I know, Gram." She stood up. "I'm going upstairs to finish some lesson plans for tomorrow. I love you." She hugged Alma. "Thanks for caring."

Upstairs, Ruth took out her Bible and turned to the psalm. " 'Except the LORD build the house, they labour in vain that build it,' " she read aloud. She looked up from the book. "I do want You to build my house, Lord," she whispered, "but I'm confused. I know You're in control, but with the world in such a terrible mess, it doesn't look like it. Didn't people in the war zones have faith and pray, too? The Nakamuras did, and look where they are. You'll have to help me, Lord. What I believe doesn't seem to fit with the world's reality anymore. Intellectually I know what's true. It's just harder to have the same trust when evil seems to be taking over."

She put the Bible down and picked up a reading text. "Everything seemed so much simpler six months ago, even my beliefs." She opened the text and began to plan the lesson.

six

The spring breeze was soft and mild as it whispered through the evergreen trees. Sunny dandelions glowed from the lawn, and primroses poked their heads through the soft earth by the porch. "Finish weeding along the house there, Ruth, and then go inside to do your work. I'll get these weeds and branches picked up," George instructed as they worked in the Nakamuras' yard one afternoon.

Ruth looked up. "What will happen to their fruit trees, Grandpa? Nak took such good care of them. His cherries and apples were so excellent they always got top prices."

George stopped, his arms full of trimmings. "Men from the church'll organize work teams to take care of the orchards, and we'll have some family workdays when harvest comes. Pastor Cameron set up an account for the profits so the Nakamuras'll have something to use when they start over."

Ruth nodded. "That's only right. They were always the first ones to help someone else."

"Won't be bad with everyone pitching in." He turned toward the pile of trimmings he had accumulated.

Ruth pulled the last of the grass from among the rhododendrons and azaleas. She stood and brushed dirt from her hands. "I'll be inside if you need me."

She let herself in the house and went to work on the kitchen, enjoying the warm atmosphere and humming as she worked. She pushed the mop over the kitchen floor and turned to dust carefully around the Bible, then stopped to stare at it.

"You about done?" Her grandfather stepped through the kitchen door.

"Almost," she answered. "Come over here, Grandpa. This is strange. Every time I come here the Bible's turned to a different page. At first I thought it was the wind, but the door and windows haven't been open. No one else has been in here. I'm the only one with a key."

George leaned over the table.

"See." Ruth pointed. "It's open to Numbers 2. When Suzi left, it was Psalm 23. And it's been open to other books. I can't see that anyone's been in here. Besides, who would break in to read the Bible?"

George shook his head. "It's a mystery to me." He glanced around. "Things look okay in here." He moved to the door. "Fluffy around?"

"She stays at our place since Grandma's been feeding her so well."

"She's well fed all right. Something got three of Billy's pigeons, and it was probably Fluffy. Don't know how she got in or out, though. The cage was all locked up."

"I hope no one's playing pranks. People still have it in for this place—and anyone connected with it."

"We'll keep our eyes on things. Let's go home, Ruth. Men from church'll finish up."

⁂

As they walked into the kitchen, Alma looked up from the stove and wiped her hands on her apron. Enticing aromas rose from kettles bubbling on the stove. "I need one of you to run down to Bob's market and pick up a few items for me. If you want supper, that is."

"Smells good enough now," George said as he raised a lid and sniffed.

"No, you don't, George Peterson. Keep the lid on that kettle!" Alma quickly took the lid from him and replaced it.

"But I'm a good taster, Alma, my dear. Such torture you put a man through."

"If you were out in the barn where you belong right now, you wouldn't be tortured. Out!" Alma winked at Ruth as she attempted a scowl at her husband.

George left the room, rubbing his stomach and sniffing

the delicious aromas.

"They say the way to a man's heart's through his stomach. Sure works with George," Alma declared with a twinkle in her eye as she checked her kettles.

"I'll go, Grandma. What do you need?" Ruth asked and reached for her car keys.

Alma handed her the list and money. "Enjoy the drive, dear. We'll be walking everywhere once gasoline is rationed."

❧

The bell above the door jangled as Ruth entered Fir Glen Market. All the spare wall space in the small country store was covered with war-related posters. "Man the guns. Join the navy!" a poster declared. "It's a woman's war, too! Join the Waves." A new grouping encouraged their efforts on the home front: "Conserve everything you have. Raise and share food."

"What can I do for you, Ruth?" Bob Miller stood behind the counter in the large grocer's apron that enveloped his small frame.

Ruth selected the items on her grandmother's list and placed her purchases on the counter. Bob rocked back and forth on his heels and pursed his lips as he surveyed her selections. "Where's your empty toothpaste tube?"

"My empty what?" Ruth asked, puzzled.

"Toothpaste tube. Can't let you buy any more toothpaste unless you turn in your empty tube. They're war materials now, you know," he informed her smugly. "Government regulations."

"I hadn't heard about that one." She put the toothpaste back. "Next time." She scanned the list. "How's the job of air-raid warden?" she asked, making conversation.

"Well," Bob rocked up on his toes, "most people are pretty careful about covering their windows at night, but I've got some I'll have to get tough with." He stuck his thumbs under his apron straps. "Old man Jones is one. Sneaks around, too. Makes a guy wonder what he's up to, especially with spies around." He jerked his head toward a poster that declared "The enemy is listening."

Ruth was relieved to hear the bell jangle as Marge stepped into the store. A bus could be heard pulling back onto the road. "If it isn't the hardworking librarian, home after a long day's work." Ruth went to greet her friend. "After next week, we'll all be riding the bus instead of driving."

Marge wrinkled her nose. "It's better than walking, but I'd rather drive. What's up?"

"Just picking up some items for Grandma—and being caught up on local gossip." Ruth jerked her head toward Bob. "A side benefit of shopping here."

"Know what you mean." They walked over to the counter. "I get off early Monday," Marge said. "Want to meet at Sandy's for a Coke after school? My folks are so busy at the shipyards no one's ever home. Mom's been promoted to. . ."

"Ahem, ladies," Bob interrupted, pointing to a poster. "Enemy agents are always near; if you don't talk, they won't hear," it read. "We must be careful what we say these days." He reached under the counter and pulled out a newspaper. "See this ad?" He held it up. "Even the FBI wants our help in catching suspicious characters. Think they'd have that ad if spies weren't everywhere?"

"We'll be more careful, Bob," Ruth assured him as she picked up her groceries and winked at her friend. "I need to get these home to Grandma. See you, Marge."

ªª

On Monday afternoon Ruth erased the penmanship examples from the blackboard and turned to the class. "Put your pens and ink bottles away," she directed, "and pass your papers to the front." A bustle of activity followed. "And remind your parents that the picnic on the last day of school is a potluck. That's next week." She looked at the class. "You're dismissed."

"Hey, Miss Sinclair, think I'll pass spelling this year?" Tim Henderson said as he hopped over to Ruth.

"If you study instead of collecting newspapers and chasing

spies. You have all summer to do that."

"No, I don't. I have to pick strawberries and beans and all that stuff. My parents said so. Hey, I've made three dollars on the papers I've collected. Haven't caught any spies yet, but we're on their trail. Me and Charlie saw lights flashing around Mr. Griffin's plant. When school's out we'll find out what it is. See ya."

Ruth smiled. *I should turn Tim loose on the mysteries at Nakamuras' place,* she thought. She put together the papers she needed to take home and added *Ben-Hur* to the pile as she left to meet Marge.

The two women settled into their favorite booth by the café window. "So, have you seen Jim lately?" Marge pried as she sipped her Coke.

"Not for the past week," Ruth answered and shifted in her seat. "He's busy at the plant, I guess."

"He likes you, I can tell." Marge grinned at her friend.

"He's just a flirt and a tease." Ruth twirled a strand of hair between her fingers and looked down at her Coke. "I am over Harold, Marge, but I can't send him a Dear John letter now. Just because Jim's here and attractive doesn't make it right to dump Harold that way."

Marge raised an eyebrow at Ruth and shook her head. "You protest too much, my dear." She wiped her mouth with a napkin. "Not to change the subject, but I need to do some shopping. Want to meet me in Brookwood Saturday? I go to lunch at 12:30. We can eat and look around a bit. I need some new lipstick." She pursed her pink lips. "Something bright."

"Sounds good." Ruth picked up her papers and followed Marge out the door. As it started to close, a man shoved past her. Ruth staggered sideways, trying not to fall. The papers went flying, and *Ben-Hur* skidded across the ground. The man grabbed the book and dashed behind the café.

Ruth regained her footing and stared after the retreating figure. "Marge, that's the man who hollered at me for being at

Suzi's. Why would he steal a book?" She started to reach for the nearest papers.

"My, my, you need to be more organized, Miss Sinclair." Jim came up behind them and bent to pick up the papers. "Or is this a new way to grade papers—throw them out and the closest ones get As?"

Ruth frowned. "Actually, it's not funny, Jim. A man pushed past me, knocking the papers and a book out of my hands. It's odd, though. He grabbed *Ben-Hur* and ran off with it."

"A literary thief? Doesn't he know we have libraries?"

"He's the man I told you about—the one who hollered at me for being at Nakamuras's. The book was one I borrowed from Suzi."

Jim walked around the back of the café. "No one here." He bent over and picked up *Ben-Hur*. "Either he's a mighty fast reader, or he didn't like the book." He handed it back to her.

"It's another attempt to intimidate me because I'm helping my Japanese friends," Ruth declared firmly.

"I've been so busy at the plant I've neglected our defense work, I'm afraid," Jim commented. "But gas rationing and scrap drives are coming up. I hope you're ready for a busy summer, Miss Sinclair."

"Once school's out, I'll have plenty of time, Jim. Just let me know." She smiled at him.

"You can count on it. Nice to see you, Marge." He touched his hand to his hat and entered the café.

"Ruth, you're crazy. That man is handsome, charming, witty, successful—you name it. And he obviously likes you. But you insist on staying loyal to a guy who doesn't even deserve it." Marge hit her palm against her forehead. "The teacher needs to go back to school."

"Come on, Miss Dramatic. You've spent too long in the romance section of your library. A walk home will clear your head." Ruth pulled Marge toward the road, but her mind was still on Jim retrieving her scattered papers.

seven

Alma bustled about the living room doing her spring-cleaning. The windows had been stripped of their lace curtains and sparkled after Alma's thorough scrubbing. She removed the cushions from the sofa and stacked them on the floor. "We'll have to take these outside and beat winter's dust out of them."

Ruth collected doilies from the end tables and added them to the pile of curtains. "I'll get all these washed and starched, Gram. Where do you store the frames to stretch the lace curtains? I'll put them together for you."

"In the. . . Ruth, is this your bookmark?" Alma held up a strip of paper that had fallen under a sofa cushion.

She looked up. "It's one of Suzi's. I wondered where it went. It fell out of *Ben-Hur* a while back."

Alma inspected the bookmark before handing it to Ruth. "She wrote Bible verses down one side." She chuckled. "Suzi knows the Bible better than this. There's no Psalm 638:42. And there's no Amos 34:14 either. Hmm, maybe Amy wrote them." She turned the bookmark over. "Ruth, these are lovely." Tiny colored sketches of flowers, animals, and angels covered the strip of paper.

"Suzi loved to make them," Ruth explained. "The whole family liked to read, so she made a supply of bookmarks they could all use. I felt bad to lose this one."

Alma handed it to her. "Take it upstairs, dear. And check your cake on the way. It smells mighty good. Be sure to let Grandpa know it's for the school picnic tomorrow. You know how much he likes chocolate cake!"

❧

The next morning Ruth balanced her cake in one hand and books in the other as she approached the school, where Mrs.

Foster was unlocking the front door. "Here, let me help you." Mrs. Foster hurried to let Ruth into the building. "Mmm, yummy-looking cake. Can you believe this is the last day of school? Where has the year gone?" she chatted as she walked down the hall with Ruth. "I'll hold your cake while you unlock your classroom."

Ruth pulled the door open. "Thanks, Mrs. . . Oh, what's happened?" Books were strewn all over the floor in front of the bookcases.

"Oh, my, who would do that?" Mrs. Foster set the cake on a desk and stared at the mess. "Some of them have been damaged. Mrs. Hastings needs to know about this. I'll take care of that for you."

"Thanks." Ruth took a deep breath. "I'll have a word with my class, but I'm sure it wasn't one of them." She bent to pick up a book with a broken spine. "I know I locked the room yesterday. I had to unlock it to get in this morning. How did someone get in?" She stared at the mess.

"Hey, Miss Sinclair." Tim bounded into the room. "I came early to help you get the class booth ready." He stopped when he saw the mess of books. "Hey, why are all those books on the floor?"

"I have no idea, Tim. They were there when I came in. Do you know anything about it?"

"Uh-uh. Nobody in our class would do that, Miss Sinclair." Tim's face brightened. "It's a mystery. Hey, me and Charlie'll be on the case." Tim got down on the floor and looked carefully among the books. "I'm looking for clues, Miss Sinclair."

"I feel better now, Tim." Ruth smiled and glanced at her watch. "I need to set up our class booth. When you're done, come out to the gym and help me. We'll clean this up after Mrs. Hastings looks into it." She turned to straighten her desk.

"Sure thing." Tim got up and inspected the door, then moved to the windows at the side of the room. "Hey, Miss Sinclair, this window's not closed! See!" He pointed to a middle window that was slightly ajar.

Ruth stared at the window and shuddered. "That's how some-one got in! But why?" She looked at the mess again and shook her head. "We'll take care of this later. I have to get to the gym. Don't disturb anything till Mrs. Hastings has been here."

Tim nodded.

Ruth hurried to the gym to find it transformed into a school carnival. The PTA had draped streamers and set up booths along the sides where the classes would sponsor games. A fishing booth offered prizes for the younger children while a ball toss was set up for the older ones. Near the piano, chairs were arranged in a circle for a cakewalk. A bingo game and the ring toss completed the games along that wall. Down the center of the room, the Women's Club had added three booths that offered prizes for tossing buttons into saucers, dropping clothespins into bottles, and pinning the tail on the donkey.

There was a bustle of activity in the room as Ruth walked over to the ring toss booth. "Milk bottles, rings, the sign, box of prizes. It's all here." She spaced the milk bottles around the table.

"Hey, Miss Sinclair, is our class doing the ring toss?" Tim bounded over, picked up a ring, and tossed it toward the glass bottles. It ricocheted off and dropped at Ruth's feet. She bent to pick it up.

"A fifth- and sixth-grade tradition, Tim. Here, help me put up our sign." Ruth held one end while Tim grabbed the other.

"Hey, Mr. Griffin," Tim waved and called out as he spied Jim coming into the gym.

Jim looked around at the array of activities and waved back. He stopped to chat here and there as he walked over to them. "Mighty impressive booth you've got there." He picked up a ring and tossed it. It spun around the neck and settled on the bottle. "So, what do I win, Miss Sinclair? How about din-ner Friday night?" He glanced at her and grinned.

"Enough of you, Mr. Griffin. I'll have to put you to work to keep you in line." She put the ring back and shook her finger at him.

Jim put his hands up in defense. "Actually I'm leaving, but I need to borrow your assistant. I'm in charge of the softball game, and I need Tim to show me where the equipment's kept. Okay, Tim?"

"Sure thing, Mr. Griffin." Tim bounded out of the booth. "Oh, hey, I found a clue to the crime."

Jim's eyebrows shot up. "Crime? What crime?" He looked from one to the other.

Ruth explained the situation she had walked into that morning.

"I'm investigating it," Tim declared. "Me and Charlie are solving mysteries. We're checking on the lights around your plant, too, Mr. Griffin."

Jim frowned and jingled the coins in his pocket. "What do you mean, Tim, lights around the plant?" He stared at Tim intently.

"Me and Charlie saw lights—like flashlights—blinking around your plant. I live down the road from there, you know. Me and Charlie play outside after dark, and we saw the lights. When school's out we're gonna see if it's spies."

"You'd better let me handle it, Tim. I'm glad you told me." He ruffled Tim's hair. "Come on; let's get set up before the bell rings." Jim walked off with his arm around Tim's shoulders.

Ruth tidied the booth and hurried back to her classroom as the tardy bell rang and the children made a noisy dash for their seats. "Class, quiet down. I need to talk to you." She looked around at their faces. She knew them all well. The boys could be noisy and mischievous, but not one would cause any damage. "When I came in this morning, all the books were out of the bookcases and on the floor. Does anyone know anything about it?"

They looked at the mess on the floor, at each other, and then back at her. Heads shook no.

"If you hear anything, let me know."

They nodded and wiggled in their seats, anxious to get on with the morning's activities.

"Before we clean up, I need a word with the Junior Volunteers. Over the summer you'll have a lot to do to help the war effort. Tim will be your captain. He'll notify you about meetings and what needs to be done. Be sure to wear your badges so people will know you're official." She looked around the room. "Any questions?"

Mike raised his hand. "What'll we do?"

"Continue to collect newspapers. Also, the government needs milkweed floss to use in life preservers. It looks like this." Ruth held up a sample from the display Jim had given her. "And you can collect foil from gum wrappers. You'll be paid fifty cents for a large ball."

A buzz ran through the room. "Fifty cents, wow!" John exclaimed.

"Take all this to the feed store," Ruth concluded. "Now, let's clean out the desks. Mrs. Hastings investigated the problem of the bookcase, so Tim and Charlie can put the books back on the shelves. Cynthia, Betty, and Alice will clean the back cabinets. I'll be by to check your desks."

The room was a bustle of activity as the children packed up their belongings to take home for the summer, and the wastebasket grew full of old papers. Finally Ruth clapped her hands. "Take your seats, class. The room looks great."

With a noisy scurry the students returned to their desks and sat impatiently. She nodded at them. "You're excused to the gym for the carnival." As they dashed for the door, she called out, "Don't run!" They slowed to a fast, long-strided walk. Ruth followed with her cake. "Slow down, John!"

"That's like telling a hurricane to slow down, Miss Sinclair," Jim commented as he met her at the door. "Umm, cake looks good." He reached his finger toward the frosting, and Ruth slapped at his hand. He feigned a hurt look. "What's the agenda for today?"

"The carnival till lunch. Afterwards, your softball game for the older kids and outdoor games for the younger ones." She waited while he opened the door.

"Sounds great. I'm on my way back to work. See you at noon. I don't want to miss the picnic!"

"If you promise to keep your fingers out of the frosting, would you drop my cake off at the grove on your way? I need to get to the gym."

"Only if I get the first piece. The way to a man's heart, you know." He winked and grinned as he took the cake and walked off.

Ruth hurried to the gym and the class booth, where a line had already formed, waiting impatiently for her arrival. The games began, and the morning passed quickly as the children enjoyed the booths and the prizes they won.

As she waited for more customers, Ruth overheard a group of boys arguing nearby. "Our side'll beat you. Mr. Griffin showed me how to pitch."

"Uh-uh, will not. He coached us good. We can hit that ball clear out of the field."

"Mr. Griffin said. . ." The group ambled on to another game.

She smiled to herself. *Jim's certainly made a hit with the boys around here. He's been a strong Christian influence on them, too.* She sighed. *If I hadn't made that promise to Harold, what would my life be now?* She watched the buzz of activity around her. A small girl squealed and jumped up and down at a prize she'd won. *I'd be dating Jim Griffin, is what I'd be doing,* she said to herself. *Why did I give in when Harold told me he was going overseas? Would breaking up then really have been worse? When I compare Harold and Jim. . .*

She glanced at her watch. Her head was ringing from the piano tunes Mrs. Foster had been playing all morning for the cakewalk and the noisy chatter and squeals of the children. "Tim," she called out, "would you be in charge of closing down our booth? Get some others to help you. I have to help set out the food." Ruth brought out boxes in which to pack the items.

"Sure thing, Miss Sinclair," Tim replied and went to round up some classmates.

She hurried to the grove of fir trees behind the school, where picnic tables were set up, and began cutting cakes and pies. Mothers were setting out an array of food on long tables—mounds of potato salad, platters of sandwiches and fried chicken, and bowls of shimmering Jell-O.

"The war hasn't affected the potluck spirit, I see," Jim commented as he approached the tables laden with food and eyed the enticing selection. "I do love potlucks!"

"These pies and cakes won't be as sweet as they used to be, but I doubt there will be much left anyway." Ruth cut the last cake and set it with the other desserts.

The noon bell rang, and with shouts and whoops the children raced to the grove, shoving and pushing to be first in line. She watched as Jim stepped over to the line and stood with his hands on his hips, staring at them. The roughhousing ceased, and they settled down to wait their turns.

He walked back to Ruth as she finished cutting the last pie. "Join me for lunch? I have a few things to bring up about civilian defense." He began to fill his plate, taking some of each dish till his plate overflowed.

Ruth nodded. "My feet will be thankful to rest awhile."

They found a place at the end of a table. Jim put his plate down and bowed his head briefly, then tackled his food. Ruth sat a moment in surprise. *Harold would never have done that in public,* she thought. *Why do I keep comparing the two?*

"You're not hungry?" Jim asked, bringing her back to the meal. "This is tremendous!" He smiled at her warmly.

And this is crazy, she thought. *I'm blushing. I feel as silly as Cynthia Richards when Billy Benton chases her. Calm down, Ruth. You're a teacher, not a kid.* She looked around. Certain her red face was obvious to everyone, she bent over her plate. "Starved," she replied. "I was just thinking about the year. So much has happened since last fall."

Jim put down his chicken bone. "The war sure has changed the world," he agreed as he tackled his dessert.

Ruth ate the last bite on her plate. "Now, what is the civilian defense business we need to discuss?"

Jim finished his piece of cherry pie. "Tart is good," he muttered through puckered lips and pushed his plate away. "This really is business and not a date. Scout's honor. A week from Saturday there's a civilian defense meeting in Portland. It's important we both be there."

"What's it about?"

"Rallying community support for the war effort. There's a lot of activity coming up, and we need to be prepared. So, it's a date? No, sorry, wrong choice of words. You'll go?"

Ruth nodded. She picked up her plate and reached for his. "But right now I have to help clean up, and you're wanted on the ball field."

A group of boys rushed up to their table with bats, balls, and mitts. "Come on, Mr. Griffin. Time for the game!"

Jim rose to his feet, groaning. "Don't I get time to rest after all this food I ate?"

"Nooo," the group chorused. "Play ball!"

Ruth carried the plates, her heart pounding. *This is not a date,* she reminded herself. *Get your mind focused on the reality of your situation, Ruth Sinclair, and get your heart back in control. You'll only cause it a lot of pain.*

She watched Jim on the ball field, surrounded by an excited group of boys. *They've found a great hero. He may not be overseas risking his life, but he's sure making a difference in the lives of these kids.* She fought a stab of sadness as she watched him start the game. Her mind drifted to the defense meeting. A whole day together. . . She shook her head. *Come on, Ruth, get busy with the dishes. You got yourself in this pickle. Now you'll have to live with it.*

eight

The aroma of fresh bread filled the kitchen as Alma took a loaf from the oven. "Mmm, smells good, Grandma." Ruth entered the kitchen and sat down at the table. "Got your list ready? I'd better get going, or I'll miss the bus and be late meeting Marge for lunch."

Alma wiped her hands on her apron and looked over her list. "The material for the banner, thread. Oh, and some seeds. We need to get the rest of the garden in." She jotted down the items she needed and handed Ruth the list.

"Walking and riding the bus will take a bit of getting used to." Ruth picked up her purse. "With gasoline rationing, our lives aren't the same." She paused at the door. "Well, I'm off. I'm thankful we're only a half mile from the bus stop, Gram."

੩

As Ruth waited for the bus in front of Fir Glen Market, she looked around at her world. It looked the same, but it wasn't. Joe's Feed Store on the corner was now used to spot enemy planes. Arlan's gas station on the other corner was rationing gasoline. The school across the road organized children to collect materials to fight the war. "And beyond the school is the Griffin Container Company that produces cans for Bird's-Eye Foods and brought Jim Griffin back home to complicate my life," she muttered aloud.

A horn beeped in front of her, and she looked up to see the bus waiting. She handed the driver her ticket and took a seat toward the front. *Even the bus is a reminder of war,* she thought as she noted the men in uniform, accounting for most of the passengers. The bus pulled into the depot in Brookwood where groups of servicemen waited for buses to their destinations.

I'll get Gram's material before I meet Marge, she said to herself and headed down the block toward Penney's.

Her heart gave a funny turn as she watched the couple ahead of her. A bobby-soxer in plaid skirt and saddle shoes walked with her little finger linked to that of a guy in a letterman's sweater. That had been Harold and her. As the couple turned into the malt shop where the high school crowd still gathered, she wondered what the future held for them—and for her.

In Penney's she paid for her grandmother's material, then headed for Woolworth's and lunch with Marge. As she entered the five-and-dime store, a hand waved at her from the lunch counter.

"What are you having?" Marge asked Ruth quickly, then twirled her stool around to give the waitress their order. "I'm so excited! I got a letter from Jack. He's stationed in California now, you know. He misses me terribly and wants to get married as soon as he comes home on leave. You'll have to help me plan the wedding!"

The waitress brought their food, and Marge nibbled on her hot dog as she chatted about dresses and flowers. "You'll be my maid of honor, so I need your honest opinion. What do you think of that combination? Ruth, are you listening?"

"What color was that?" Ruth asked. "I was daydreaming, I guess." She took a bite of her sandwich.

"Umm, telltale sign. You never did that till Jim Griffin came around. I see signs of infatuation, Miss Sinclair," Marge said smugly. She glanced at her watch. "If we get going I have time to buy some makeup. You done?"

"All set; lead the way." Ruth collected her package and purse and followed her friend to the makeup section.

Marge picked up a tube of red Tangee lipstick. "I love these bright colors! Or do you like the shade of this Maybelline better? I can't decide. See if you can find a sample." They rummaged through the tiny samples for the right shades.

"We probably won't see these samples much longer if the

war continues," Ruth remarked. "Every week some item becomes scarce."

"Speaking of scarce, if you see any bobby pins, let me know. They're hard to get now. Rolling my hair up on rags just isn't the same." Marge wrinkled her nose as she made her selections and got in line to pay for them. "Waiting in line is becoming another national pastime," she grumbled. The line inched slowly toward the cash register.

"So, Miss Sinclair," Marge pried, "how are things going with Jim? Any progress?"

Ruth felt herself blush and looked down quickly so Marge wouldn't notice. "We're just friends, Marge. Now that I'm on vacation, defense work will pick up, I'm sure."

"Good, good." Marge grinned. "I was afraid I'd have to work at getting you two together, but this way I can just let nature take its course." She found herself at the cashier and put her items on the counter. "Do you ever get bobby pins in anymore?" she inquired.

The cashier stopped, put her hand on her hip, and stared at Marge. "Don't you know there's a war on?" she snapped. She slowly rang up the purchases, handed the change to Marge, and smacked her gum before turning to the next customer.

"I remember when clerks were helpful and had manners," Ruth commented dryly as they walked away. "It's the war again. Not enough workers to go around, so nobody worries about getting fired anymore."

Marge glanced at her watch. "Gotta run," she declared. "The library waits for no one. Thanks for coming in, Ruth." She checked her purchases and hurried away.

Ruth shifted her parcel. *Only seeds to go,* she thought and headed for the garden supplies. *Why am I feeling so melancholy? Snap out of it, Ruth. Think how blessed you are to be in America, safe and sound.*

Back on the sidewalk, she passed a record shop filled with high school kids listening to the latest songs. A melody drifted out the door. "There'll be bluebirds over the white cliffs of

Dover. . ." She paused to listen. *The same English cliffs Harold's been flying over with the RAF,* she thought. *Fighting the Nazis is so dangerous. I pray he's safe.* She walked on and stopped at the end of the block to check the traffic.

As she crossed the street, Jim Griffin stepped out of the county clerk's office. Her heart gave a funny thump as she walked up to him. "Hi, Jim. Busy on defense business?"

His face brightened into a smile. "The teacher on vacation! Just the person I want to see. We have lots of work ahead of us this summer." He cocked his eyebrow in the way that had become so familiar. "We'll have to spend hours and hours working together. I like that idea—friend." He chuckled.

Ruth shook her head. "You're impossible."

He glanced at her packages. "I see you bought out the town."

"No, just some material and seeds for Grandma. I had lunch with Marge."

A fine mist began to drift down softly but steadily. "Good old Oregon mist. We'd better find some shelter. Did you drive in?" he asked.

"With gas rationing? You must be checking up on me. No, it's these feet and the bus from now on, I'm afraid." Ruth held a package over her head as the mist came down.

"Then I'll offer you a ride home. I'm on official business, and you work for me, so the gas is provided." Jim smiled at her warmly.

"I gladly accept, boss."

"This way." He took her elbow and led her to his car. The mist continued as they got in and headed out of town.

"So, how do you like being back in Oregon and working at the plant?" Ruth asked him.

"It's good to be back. I knew I'd run the plant one day, so I wanted a chance to be on my own for a while first. When the war started, it was time to settle down and do my part." Jim looked over at her. "And you. Where are you heading in life, Ruth? What's important to you?"

The mist came faster on the windshield, and the wiper blades moved with a rhythmic whish and thump. "I enjoy being a teacher and guiding the children. It's like a calling, I guess."

Jim nodded. "I know what you mean. That's what I feel in working with the youth at church. God has done so much for me; I need to pass it on."

"Have you always been a Christian, Jim?" Ruth looked over at him.

"I was raised in a Christian home, but in college the world seemed pretty attractive. When I moved to California, I felt God could wait for a later day. I wanted my version of fun and success first. It was the war that got to me. That and John Kensington, a guy I worked with."

"What do you mean?" She looked puzzled.

"John was a strong Christian, but his faith wasn't just some beliefs he memorized or a list of rules." He paused. "The way he lived made his faith seem so real. He was what he believed."

The mist turned to a steady rain, running in rivulets down the side windows.

Jim drummed his fingers on the steering wheel. "For a long time, I had wrestled with the way God runs the world. It didn't make sense and wasn't how I'd have done it. And I didn't like someone telling me what to do, even if He was God. Then I met John and saw it all differently. He got me into Bible study, too. I even took some classes at a Bible college."

He pulled up to a stop sign and shifted. The car was quiet for a moment before he continued. "I have to admit I didn't take God seriously when I was younger. It was just something I did. But when the Japanese attacked Pearl Harbor, I really woke up. You see, a good friend of mine was killed in that attack. I realized how fragile life is and who's ultimately in control."

"You didn't get bitter at the Japanese, like some people around here?"

Jim shook his head. "No, God deals with us as individuals,

so that's how I have to deal with people. I'm not perfect, and God still loves me, so I have to give others that, too. And not all Japanese are against America."

He turned down Woodland Avenue, and they rode in comfortable silence. "Here we are," Jim said as he pulled into the Peterson driveway. He reached into his briefcase and took out several papers. "Type these for me?"

"Sure thing, boss." Ruth took the papers. "I'll drop them by the plant when they're done." She put the packages over the papers to protect them from the rain.

"Thanks for all your help, Ruth. I appreciate what you do for me—and for our country. I. . ." Jim paused and put his hand over Ruth's. "I. . .uh. . ." He seemed to be searching for the right words and squeezed her hand gently. "I'm glad you volunteered for this job," he said softly.

Ruth looked away from his tender gaze, not trusting the emotions stirring in her heart. She took a deep breath and opened the car door. "Thanks for the ride, Jim. See you later." She closed the door and dashed to the house as the rain poured down.

The house was quiet when Ruth stepped inside. She left the packages for her grandmother on the kitchen table and walked into the living room, stopping at the window to watch the rain. "I've done it," she said out loud. "I'm falling for Jim Griffin. He's everything I want and admire in a man, but I feel so guilty. Even though I think he's what God would want for me, I wasn't brought up to dump someone who's risking his life in a war." She paced the room.

"God, what do I do? I feel so torn. This rain is me inside." She cried softly. With a sigh she sat down and bowed her head. "Lord, I feel trapped. Show me Your will and direction for my life. I don't want to go back on my word to Harold or hurt him when he's off fighting for his country, but my heart isn't with him anymore. Please help me!"

nine

Ruth woke to the sound of pots and pans banging in the kitchen. She dressed quickly and hurried downstairs. As she poked her head through the door, Alma was noisily putting the utensils back in the cupboard. "Is this your new alarm clock, Grandma?" she teased as she walked in.

Her grandmother paused. "Morning, Ruth. Sorry I woke you so early. I couldn't sleep any longer." She plopped into a chair with a sigh, wiping her hands on her apron. "It's that Velma Miller. Nobody gets under my skin like she does."

Ruth chuckled and poured two cups of coffee. "What's she done this time?" She placed one cup in front of her grandmother.

Alma's fingers drummed on the table. "Her women's club does a lot of good, I'll grant you that, but she has to run everything. As you know, our Ladies Aid is making quilts and collecting clothes for the English refugees. We're sending them through the church's relief agencies. Now Velma's gone and promised it all to the Red Cross without asking anyone. And she didn't even help us. If she'd come to church more than once or twice a year, she'd know what's going on."

"She does have a lot of nerve." Ruth got up. "Come on, Grandma. You need to work out your frustrations." Ruth opened the back door and looked out. "The rain's cleared, and it's a perfect day to plant the rest of the garden. I'll help you." She stepped outside into the crisp morning air.

Ruth collected the rake and hoe while Alma retrieved the seeds and string. "We'll start over here where I left off," Alma said as she surveyed the garden. She bent over to pull a weed.

"Ouch! I still can't do that, Gram." Ruth watched as Alma bent over, legs straight and hands to the ground. "That makes my legs ache!"

Alma laid her hands flat on the ground and grinned up at Ruth. "Don't tell me you're too old," she teased. "Must be my second childhood that does it." She straightened and stood with her hands on her hips.

"I couldn't do that in my first childhood. Must be Dad's side," Ruth declared as she picked up the hoe and dug a shallow trench for her grandmother's seeds.

The air was fresh after the rain. A robin hopped along the ground, looking for worms, and a meadowlark warbled from a nearby tree. "I think heaven must be an eternal spring, Grandma; it's so lovely." The fragrance of spring blossoms wafted on the gentle breeze that rustled the leaves. Ruth breathed deeply and turned back to her work.

Alma scanned the garden, planning the remaining rows in her mind. "I want several plantings of beans. Let's leave room here for another row later." She bent to drop seeds in the row Ruth had prepared. They worked quietly, enjoying the chorus of birds in the nearby trees.

"You ladies do a fine job." George called out as he stopped at the end of the garden. "I could watch you work all morning."

Alma straightened and put her hands on her hips. "If you have that much spare time, George Peterson, you can clean the henhouse!"

"Nope. Been working with Joe over at Nakamuras' and came to get a saw. Say, Ruth, it's odd. Went to feed Billy's pigeons and now there are ten. Did you have a talk with Fluffy and get her to put those three back?"

"I'm afraid not, Grandpa." Ruth frowned. "Someone's messing with things over there. The community was so upset when the place was ransacked; maybe someone's resorting to more subtle mischief instead. Anything to get back at us and make us uncomfortable over there."

"As long as nothing's hurt I guess there isn't anything we can do. It's odd though." He turned. "I'll get what I need and go back over."

Alma picked up her string. "That's enough for now, Ruth. I

have bread rising and need to get back to it. And the Ladies Aid meets this afternoon. We're sorting clothes we can repair for the refugees."

She walked to a round seedbed and bent over to pull a weed. "Flowers are slow coming up this year. Must be all the rain. The zinnias and marigolds are so colorful when it's brown and dry in the summer. I hope they do well."

Ruth collected the rake and hoe and put them away. "I'll get cleaned up and walk down to Bob's market, Gram. I have a couple notices to post for Jim. We can finish the garden this evening. Need anything while I'm there?"

Alma shook her head and headed for the house.

❧

The morning sun had warmed the air when Ruth left for the market. "God's nugget," she murmured. "Walking isn't as convenient, but I'd have missed this beauty if I'd been driving." Fields along the gravel road were a carpet of green. Wildflowers poked their heads up here and there, adding an array of color to the scene.

The bell over the door jangled as she entered the store. "Good morning, Mrs. Edwards," Ruth greeted a customer and walked to the bulletin board. Bob hurried over to read the notices Ruth was posting.

"Got to keep track of what goes up here," he said. "This is an official board, you know." He lowered his voice. "I think old man Jones is up to no good. Someone said his neighbor's cousin saw him sneaking around the Nakamura place. He's always been the sneaky sort. Won't cooperate either."

"What's he done?" Ruth's mind tried to imagine old man Jones pulling the pranks at Suzi's. It didn't fit.

"It's them chicken houses of his. Won't keep the lights off at night. Says he's allowed to keep 'em on so his hens'll lay. Uses 'em to signal the enemy, I say." He rocked back on his heels, his thumbs hooked in his suspenders. He leaned closer and looked around. "Rumors are the Griffin plant's been converted to war production. Don't know what they'd make instead of them cans. Bullets, maybe? It's all hush-hush. Arlan says a lot of trucks come and go, and they have a guard now."

The bell clanged as a woman entered the store. Bob stood back, his finger to his lips. "Keep an eye out for old man Jones. He's up to no good." He turned to his customer. "Hello, Mrs. Wilson. May I help you?" he asked cheerily.

Ruth removed an expired notice from the bulletin board and slipped out the door while Bob was occupied with his customer. "Shopping at Bob's is always an experience," she muttered as she hurried around the corner of the building and ran headlong into a large figure.

"Oh, I'm sorry. I didn't look where I was going!" she exclaimed and looked up to see the smiling face of Herschel Owens. *Oh, no,* she thought with a sinking feeling as he continued to smile at her.

"No harm done, Miss Sinclair. And how are you this fine day?" He pulled a grayish handkerchief from the pocket of his rumpled jacket and wiped his brow.

She stepped back, mumbled a "Fine, how are you?" and tried to edge around him.

"Fine, fine," he responded as he tried to pull his jacket together over his large waistline. "Mother and I haven't seen you in our store, Miss Sinclair. Being single and all, you should come in to consider some of our furniture. We have some lovely new pieces. Mother selected them herself so they should suit a lady like yourself."

Lovely furniture, my foot! she thought. *Trader's Corner is full of old junk no one would want.* She forced a smile. "Greet your mother for me."

"I will, I will. She felt poorly this morning, the dear soul, but she insisted on helping at the store, weak as she was. Wouldn't you say that's a fine mother's love?"

Fine mother's love, ha! She'd be more at home running a chain gang! Ruth grumbled to herself. "I need to be on my way, Mr. Owens," she responded briefly. She stepped around him and tried to hurry away.

"Herschel, my dear, it's Herschel to you." He continued to smile at her, then turned and walked to the door of the market.

She heard the bell jangle as she headed for the road. *There's something about him—oily, I guess I'd call it.* She gave a shudder and hurried toward home.

&

Alma looked up from her ironing as Ruth walked in. "So, what's new from gossip central?" She unplugged the iron. Without waiting for an answer she went on, "Ready for lunch? Grandpa's not back yet. We may as well eat."

Ruth took a loaf of bread from the drawer. "Sounds good. I'll make a couple extra sandwiches and take them over to him. He gets so busy he forgets to stop. I need to check on the house anyway. I worry about what's going on over there." She sliced the fresh loaf. "About the rumors. With Bob you never know how much is fact. He says the Griffin plant is producing war materials and even has a guard. His latest target is old man Jones. He thinks he's a spy." She placed thick slices of home-cured ham on the bread.

"That poor old man. He is a bit odd, but he's no spy. Since he lost his family in a house fire years ago, he hasn't been the same. I've always felt sorry for him," Alma said as she put the ironing board away and joined Ruth for lunch. They ate quietly, remembering the tragedy that had occurred down the road from them.

"Suzi looked out for him when she was here," Ruth added. "I don't think he talked to anyone else." She got up and cleared the table, then wrapped the sandwiches for her grandfather. "I'll be back soon, Gram."

She crossed the field and followed the sound of her grandfather's saw to the orchard where he was pruning limbs. "Time to eat, Grandpa. I brought some sandwiches." She put the basket down. "After lunch I'll haul those branches away for you."

"Appreciate it." He sat down on a stump and took the sandwich Ruth offered. "Things sure grow up if you don't keep at 'em. Joe had to run, but other men from the church will be over later. Thought I'd get a start. Kind of enjoy it." The smell of sawdust and damp earth hung in the air.

"I wonder how Suzi and her family are. I try to imagine how I'd feel in their situation." Ruth shuddered.

"They'll be okay. God gives strength at times like that." George took a bite of his sandwich and looked around at the peaceful orchard. "Newspaper says our men sank four Japanese carriers at Midway Island. Maybe this war's turning around." He stood up and wiped his brow. "Well, back to work. After you clean up the branches, go in and check the house while I finish trimming."

Ruth hauled the last of the branches, then headed for the house. She unlocked the door and went in. "I wonder if. . . Oh, my, what's this?" Books lay scattered all over the floor. She hurried to the porch and hollered, "Grandpa, come here! Something's happened!" She returned to the kitchen and stared at the mess.

George rushed up the porch steps and yanked open the screen door. "What's the matter?" he called out as he hurried into the room.

"Look!" She pointed to the books. "Just like at school."

George looked around and shook his head. "Everything else looks okay. Someone up to pranks is all I can say." He stared at the books scattered over the floor.

Ruth picked up several books and began returning them to the shelf. "Someone doesn't like our friendship with the Nakamuras, and they're not letting us forget it," she declared. "They want to make us so uncomfortable here they scare us away. Remember the man who hollered at me from that old car a few months ago?"

George nodded and turned at the door. "It's a puzzle, all right. Keep your eyes open, Ruth, and be careful. I'll mention it to the sheriff. Maybe he can keep an eye on the place." He stepped out on the porch and paused. "But we won't desert our friends." He left to collect his tools.

Ruth put the rest of the books back on the shelves. "How

do they get in?" she fussed. "I'm supposed to have the only key. If they want to mess things up, why do they break in so carefully? It makes me uncomfortable. Maybe that's what they want. A lot of people are looking for empty places to live these days. Housing's scarce. If they can scare us away, they'll have a place to live. But as Grandpa said, we won't be scared off!"

She locked the door carefully and joined her grandfather for the walk home.

ten

"You wait and see. Don will ask Beth Marshall to marry him before he goes overseas. I just know it. Matchmaker's instinct," Marge declared firmly. She and Ruth sat in their favorite booth at Sandy's Café, sipping their Cokes. "Ruth, don't you think so? Oh, Ruth." She waved her hand in front of Ruth's face.

"I guess so," she answered flatly and continued to stare at her glass.

Marge tried again. "Summer's whizzing by. We're over halfway through June already." She paused, then put her hand over Ruth's. "What's wrong? Something is; I can tell."

Ruth twirled her Coke glass with her hands and evaded Marge's prying.

"I'm not doing well on your love life, that's what," Marge declared. "And for the umpteenth time I didn't talk to Herschel Owens about you. I have better instincts than that, I hope you know."

"The problem's not my love life, Marge. I just feel melancholy. I don't know why. It must be the war. There's such terrible news on the radio every day."

"Have you seen Jim lately?" Marge inquired.

Ruth shook her head. "He's been busy."

"That's it! I'm a regular Dorothy Dix at solving people's problems. Think I can get my own advice column, too?" Marge looked smug. "I told you it was your love life. No Jim Griffin around and look what happens to you. Now, what can I do to get you two together?"

"Stop it, Marge. I can't get interested in Jim right now, and you know it. Besides, we're attending that civilian defense meeting in Portland Saturday, so you don't have to cook up something."

Marge brightened. "Great! You need a pick-me-up. I'll come over to help you get ready." She studied Ruth carefully. "Let's see. What should you wear? I'll look through my clos—"

Ruth interrupted her. "It's not a date, Marge. You don't need to fuss."

"Just try to keep me away!"

✍

"No, no, that dress is too plain," Marge declared as the two rummaged through Ruth's closet Saturday morning. "You want to look businesslike but with a zing to it. This is Jim Griffin you're going with, may I remind you!"

Ruth pulled out a two-piece navy outfit. "For the last time, this is not a date, Marge," she insisted and hung the outfit on the closet door.

"Then why are your cheeks red and you all in a dither? Tell me that, Ruth Sinclair." Marge plopped on the bed.

Ruth tossed her head and hunted through the closet for her shoes. "I just don't want to look inappropriate."

Marge rolled her eyes. "Sure, sure." She picked up a hairbrush. "Now about your hair. Let's see if. . ."

"Oh, no, you don't. I can handle that myself, Marge. If you want to do something, get the bottled stockings for me, will you? Over on the other dresser."

Marge wrinkled her nose. "These war shortages. What I wouldn't give for nylons!" She sighed and picked up the container. "Two years ago if someone had told me we'd put stocking-colored liquid all over our legs and draw a seam down the back with an eyebrow pencil, I'd have laughed my head off!"

Ruth finished dressing and put the final touches on her shoulder-length hair. "That about does it."

Marge stood back to check Ruth's appearance. "Nice, but I wish I'd brought my new lipstick—Passion Red, it's called. That would be the touch you need."

Ruth laughed. "Passion Red doesn't sound like a civilian defense meeting, Marge. Now, along with you. I don't need a chaperone."

"I'm going, I'm going. I get the hint. But you have to call me as soon as you get home."

"Out!" Ruth ordered. "It's not a date!"

The screen door slammed, and Ruth walked into the living room to wait. *I'm nervous,* she thought. *This does feel like a date, though I'd never admit it to Marge.* A knock sounded at the door. She opened it, and Jim stood there, handsome in a dark blue suit. *Just like a guy picking up a date,* she thought. *Get ahold of yourself, Ruth.*

"Ready?" Jim stepped inside as Ruth grabbed her notebook. "Mm, I'll have the best-looking assistant there." He looked her over in obvious admiration.

Ruth flushed. "You're too much, Jim Griffin."

"Just honest." He opened the car door for her, got in, and pulled out onto the road. "If we're lucky, we'll miss the shipyard traffic. That gets nasty, even on Saturday." He smiled at her. "So, how's vacation?"

Ruth settled back and relaxed. "Busy. The Victory Garden, typing for my boss, keeping up Nakamuras' place—that sort of thing." She glanced out the window as they turned onto the highway. "Oh, look, Jim." She pointed. "My favorite Burma Shave signs." She stared out the window at the series of small signs, each with part of the rhyme that advertised Burma Shave Shaving Cream.

She started to read the first sign, and Jim joined in:

Past
Schoolhouses
Take it slow
Let the little
Shavers grow.
Burma Shave

Jim laughed. "That's my favorite, too." His fingers drummed on the steering wheel as he glanced at her sideways. "So, how's the rest of your life going?"

Ruth ducked the question. "Just fine. No problems. Life's busy. This war keeps the days packed with things to do," she rambled.

He cleared his throat. "Inside of Ruth, I mean. You look distressed, I guess I'd call it."

She looked down and didn't answer.

"I don't mean to pry, but I get the feeling you and God have a cooling between you."

She turned quickly and frowned. "How can you say that, Jim? I'm in church every Sunday. I teach Sunday school, do my devotions. Are you implying I'm a heathen?"

He laughed. "Of course not. But I can sense you lack peace in your heart."

"With a war on, who does have peace anymore?" she replied with a touch of sarcasm.

He continued. "I can tell because I had the same thing, the same bit of sarcasm and feeling of helplessness. God's not running things the way I think they should be run, so I'll back away from Him."

"No, I. . ." She stopped. She stared out the window at life going on around her. People walking into shops. Cars whizzing by. All as if there were nothing wrong. No evil destroying lives and cities. No hearts in a jumble.

A car honked behind them, jolting Ruth from her thoughts. "The world shouldn't be this way, Jim. You're right. I do want God to hurry and fix it."

Jim nodded. "I know the feeling. But we seldom give up the need to do it our way unless we have to. When life gets bad enough and we can't fix it, we finally let God do what He's been waiting to do all along. Make sense?"

Ruth shifted in her seat. "Of course. I could have told you that if you'd asked, but knowing and doing are two different things. It's the doing that's getting me." She ran her fingers over the notebook in her lap. "My mind knows one thing, but my feelings want something else."

Jim slowed as the traffic thickened. "That's why God often works best in life's difficulties. We're forced to stop and listen when we can't do it all ourselves. Let God work in your life, Ruth. Trust Him."

"Sometimes it all looks so bleak, Jim. The awful war news. Worry about Bud and others I know over there. The Nakamuras. It's hard to trust when people are suffering. And on top of it I feel guilty that I don't trust."

His fingers tapped on the steering wheel as he waited at a stoplight. "Did you ever think God may be able to get more of that good stuff done if we got out of the way—or were willing channels He could use? We're too busy trying to force things our way."

She was quiet and then nodded slowly. "How can I ask God to do His will when at the same time I'm demanding He do it my way? It's hard for God to work when His own people work against Him, even in their good intentions." She nodded her head in understanding.

Jim smiled over at her.

"How did you get so wise, boss?"

He took a deep breath. "A broken heart," he said softly.

"You? Never! Not break-their-hearts Griffin."

"Yep, me. Back in California. A girl I knew there. Very pretty. Fun. Lots of parties and dancing. Then I met the friend I told you about. The Christian guy I worked with." His voice sounded far away as he remembered. "I started to change. Went to church and Bible study. She didn't like it. She wanted the parties and fun. So she told me it was God or her."

"I'm sorry, Jim," Ruth said softly.

"Talk about a struggle. I wanted God to change her, and right away. Why couldn't I have both her and Him?" He leaned his shoulder against the car door. "Lately I think I see why He didn't let me have my way." He gave her a penetrating look. "But God still works with me. I've had to accept the reality of Harold."

Ruth was flustered. "Jim, I, uh, I . . ."

"Remember this, Ruth. Our faith is often like a greenhouse plant. It's strong only as long as the environment stays just right. When evil's on the march, it becomes a time of testing, and we see the shallowness of our faith for what it is. But instead of a disaster, this is God's opportunity to strengthen and deepen it so it can survive anywhere. That's what God's doing with you."

"Hm, an opportunity instead of a failure. That's encouraging, Jim."

He smiled. "The world you've known hasn't included the horrors of war and gross evil, Ruth. It's been a shock to you and confused your trust."

She nodded thoughtfully. "I agree. Because I think the world should be straightened out, I assume that God wants to correct it my way, instantly, with a wave of His hand, too. But He may have other agendas." She smiled at him. "My mind sees this, but it may take a while to bring my heart and feelings in line. The two seem to pull in opposite directions from my head these days."

"Keep trusting Him, Ruth. God doesn't promise to prevent all the evil in the world, but He does promise to be with us in it and see us through it. We're never alone in our troubles." He turned down the block. "Now, it's a gorgeous day. There'll be a lot to learn, and we can help our country."

"Thanks, Jim; that helped." She smiled at him. "Now, let's have a good day."

He pulled in the hotel parking lot in Portland and found an empty space.

Ruth looked around. "For instance, I could spend the day shopping at Meier and Frank's Department Store while you take notes on the meetings. No? Oh, well, it's Saturday, so I'm too late for their big Friday Surprise sale anyway," she teased.

Jim took her arm and steered her in the right direction. "You're not getting away from me today, Miss."

Inside the hotel they were directed to the registration table and received their agendas. "Session 1," Ruth read, "Rallying Community Support (scrap drives, rationing), Room 135, or Air Raids and West Coast Evacuation Procedures, Room 142." She looked at Jim. "Now I know why I came along. I go to one while you go to the other."

Jim nodded.

She continued. "Session 2: Civilian Defense Officials, Room 128, or Campaigns and Rallies (war bonds, rally days), Room 102."

"But it's also the company. Can you imagine if I had to spend the day with Bob Miller?" Jim wiped his hand across his forehead in mock relief. "I'll go to the sessions on air raids and civilian defense. You go to the other two. When the sessions are over, meet me back here." With a wink he walked down the hall to his session.

The afternoon sped by as Ruth filled her notebook with ideas and information. The last session ended, and she headed back to the lobby, where Jim waited for her. "Learn anything, Teacher?" he greeted her.

"My head's swimming. I filled a notebook with some great ideas I'll tell you about on the way home."

They hurried to the car and pulled out into the traffic. "How were your sessions?" Ruth inquired as they were swallowed up in the mass of buses and cars filled with Saturday afternoon shoppers.

"Informative, but that's all I can tell you. Secret stuff, you know," he winked and turned out of the traffic snarl.

As they headed out of town, Jim suggested, "How about grabbing a bite to eat? I'm starved. Traffic should be thinned out by the time we're done, too."

"Um, sounds great. All that thinking's made me hungry," Ruth replied as he drove into a restaurant parking lot and helped her from the car.

"No business talk while we eat," Jim said as they were seated. "When I have dinner with a lovely lady, I never spoil it with business." He picked up the menu. "Try the chicken with me? It's delicious." She nodded, and he gave the waitress their order.

This isn't a date, Ruth repeated to herself as she twisted the napkin in her lap.

"And you are lovely, you know," Jim was saying. "Yes, I know—just friends—but I can still admire a lovely friend, especially one with such deep blue eyes."

"Thank you, sir." She gave a nod of her head.

The waitress arrived with their dinner, and Jim bowed his head briefly. He picked up his fork. "So what have you seen of Tim since school's out?"

"Actually I haven't seen him. He's been picking strawberries, so the paper collecting and spy catching have slowed." She smiled. "He's quite a character. And such an avid detective. I may have to put him on the trail of all the odd things happening at the Nakamuras'." She took a bite of her dinner. "Um, this chicken is delicious."

Jim looked serious. "Back to the Nakamuras'." He put down his fork and leaned toward her. "Odd things? Like what?"

Ruth related the varying number of pigeons, Bible pages turned, and books scattered. "Grandpa says it's a prankster. I think it's someone who hates the Japanese and their friends and wants to irritate us enough that we'll quit working over there. Bob Miller would say it's old man Jones."

Jim was quiet and ate slowly. "Keep your eyes open, but don't let your suspicions carry you away. There's probably a logical explanation."

On the way home, Ruth related the information she had picked up from the sessions. "We're to hold scrap drives for metals, rubber, grease, and paper. And we're to push war bonds and stamps. They want us to hold a special rally day with a parade and lots of flags and banners, and we could get some trucks to haul scraps to Bob's lot to kick it off. I thought maybe the Fourth of July. With a big picnic. What do you think?"

Jim remained quiet and lost in thought. "Jim?"

"Oh, sure, sounds great. Go ahead with your plans for it."

He drove in silence till they pulled into her driveway. He turned toward her. "Thanks for coming along," he said. "I can see you're going to be a great help." He reached for her hand. "Be careful, Ruth. I care a lot about—my friend." He looked at her tenderly, then got out and opened her door. "Hurry on in now, before I forget this was business and there can't be a good-night kiss."

She paused, hoping he'd forget, till the guilty stab came back. "Good night, Jim," she said softly and hurried inside. She closed the door and leaned against it, her heart pounding.

eleven

Alma carried a bowl of fresh strawberries into the kitchen and set it down by the sink. "They're beauties this year."

"And endless," Ruth added as she filled her bowl with more berries to clean. "We'll have a big supply canned and in the cellar for winter. Even the birds can't eat them fast enough."

Alma chuckled. "Speaking of birds, did you see the Armstrong's scarecrow? They painted a Hitler-style mustache on it, cold beady eyes, and that dark hair combed across the forehead. Even the birds should know how scary that looks!"

The screen door squeaked. George came in carrying the morning paper and plopped it on the table. "Take a look at that!" He pointed to the large black headline for June 22, 1942: JAP SUB FIRES ON OREGON.

Ruth gasped. "Oh, no, are we being attacked? What did they hit?" She quickly scanned the article as Alma looked over her shoulder.

"Praise the Lord," Alma whispered. "Nothing was hit."

"They fired seventeen rounds at the mouth of the Columbia River—Battery Russell." Ruth looked up from the paper. "Do you think they'll attack here, Grandpa?"

"We'll pray not." George sat heavily "Thought I was too old, but I'm signing up with Joe Duncan to be a plane spotter. These old eyes should be good enough for that." He pounded his fist on the table. "We need to keep that post manned!"

"Grandma. . ." Ruth turned to see her grandmother with her head bowed, praying. She could sense fear even amidst their faith and shuddered. Suddenly the war was more than projects and what happened "over there."

"Ruth, are you all right?" Her grandmother looked up, concerned. "The Lord hasn't forgotten us, and He's still in control, but we have a lot of praying to do."

"I'm okay, Grandma. It's just a good dose of reality." She took out a paper and pencil. "And this is a good time to rally community support for the war effort when everyone's had a scare."

George stood up and grabbed his hat. "I'm heading to the feed store to talk to Joe." He stopped at the door. "Keep praying."

"Oh, my, I almost forgot the berries in all the confusion." Alma sat down and began to hull strawberries, putting the stems in the bowl with the clean berries and throwing the berries in the scrap bowl. She looked up at Ruth writing furiously. "Slow down, dear. Frantic effort won't win the war." She looked at the bowls. "Oh, my, I should talk!" she exclaimed as she saw what she had done.

Ruth sighed and returned to her plans. "Right now, it helps to keep busy. Besides, I have some great ideas." She picked up the paper and turned to Alma. "And I think I can help you out, too, Grandma." She had a mischievous twinkle in her eye. "I've been planning a Fourth of July Rally Day to build support for the war effort. I'm putting Velma Miller and her women's club in charge of decorations and war-bond sales. And, I'll have her round up musicians for a band." She jotted down the note.

Alma stopped her work and looked hopeful.

Ruth looked at her grandmother smugly. "That'll keep her so busy she won't have time to take over your Ladies Aid project for now. Just see that you get your shipment out to the church relief agency by July 4!"

"Ruth Sinclair, that's good thinking. She'll be so busy she won't bother about our church project." Alma chuckled and looked relieved.

Ruth raised an eyebrow at her grandmother. "If I see to the program, will you be in charge of the food?"

"If you'll help me finish these berries." She handed Ruth a bowl. "This is the last we'll can for winter. Any more goes to Pastor Cameron's food drive."

"Grandma, do you think. . .?" The doorbell rang. "I'll get it," Ruth said as she put her bowl down. She opened the door to see Tim Henderson looking very official. He handed her a pamphlet that read "What to Do in an Air Raid."

"Hey, Miss Sinclair. I'm here representing the air-raid warden," he recited. "Read these instructions and be prepared for an air-raid drill at any time. The signal will be the school bell tolling. Cars will drive up and down the roads honking—uh, uh—three long blasts—no, three short blasts and one long. That means V for Victory." Tim caught his breath after the long spiel.

"That's quite a speech, Tim," Ruth commented. "We'll study your pamphlet and be prepared." She smiled at him and swatted a fly with the pamphlet. "Now that strawberry picking's about over, we need the help of the Junior Volunteers. We're preparing a big Fourth of July Rally. Can your group put up posters for us and be victims for the Red Cross demonstrations?"

"Victims—hey, that sounds fun, Miss Sinclair! Well, gotta go. Got lots of houses to do." He jumped down the steps and took off on his bike.

Ruth sat down in the living room to study the pamphlet. "What is it, dear?" her grandmother asked as she came into the room.

"Information on air-raid drills. At the signal, we're to lie flat under a solid table, it says. And we're to be sure we have no lights showing." She handed the pamphlet to Alma.

"Looks like that Japanese attack yesterday got Bob going," Alma commented. She put the pamphlet down. "Let's get these berries done and clean up the kitchen."

When they had finished, Ruth sat down at the table with her notebook. "The Red Cross will put on a first aid demonstration. Jim will speak on what needs to be done. I'll get trucks lined up and organize the parade." She sat back, pleased with the plans. "I need to be sure people are doing their jobs, and then we're all set."

❧

The next morning she completed her phone calls. "I need to ask Pastor Cameron to have a prayer," she said aloud. "Oh, and check with Tim to see if he has volunteers for the first aid drill. And I need to round up some scraps to start off the drive." She made a note.

The day flew by. Plans were going well, and the volunteers were doing their jobs. Ruth walked into the kitchen. "Helping you with dinner will be a relief after all that. I'll peel the potatoes, Grandma."

When George came in from his chores, dinner was on the table. "It's good to sit awhile," Alma sighed as she bowed her head for grace. She looked up and passed the mashed potatoes. "I'm sorry dinner is so late. This has been quite a week."

As they finished the meal, Ruth brought out Alma's strawberry shortcake. "Mm, Alma, my dear, you're a wonder. No one would know there's any rationing, we eat so well." George smiled fondly at his wife as he relished his dessert. He patted his stomach. "I'm not sure I can even make it to my chair to finish the paper. If you ladies will excuse me, I'll go see if the world's still here." He headed for his paper and favorite overstuffed chair in the living room.

"I'll clean up in here, Grandma. Go in and sit with Grandpa. You deserve a rest after all the canning you've done."

Ruth had cleared the table and put the last of the dishes away when she heard the bong, bong of the school bell followed by a loud honking of car horns. She hurried into the living room.

"What in the world. . .?" George began.

"It's an air-raid drill!" Ruth hollered above the noise. "Turn off all the lights and lie flat under the dining room table. I'll go under the kitchen table." She hurried about switching off lights and crawled under the table.

The school bell fell silent, and the car horns sounded farther and farther away. "How long do we stay here, Ruth?" George called out.

"Till the all-clear signal. It should be anytime."

The minutes ticked by in the dark and silent house. A mild evening breeze rustled the curtains at the open windows and blew gently through the screen door to cool the house, still warm from the day's canning.

After twenty minutes, she heard her grandfather moving about in the living room. "That's enough of that," he declared. "I don't hear any bombs, so. . ."

Pow! pow! Rapid gunfire followed by breaking glass and angry shouts sounded through the open front door. Ruth hurried into the room.

"You don't suppose this was the real thing, do you?" Alma froze in confusion.

George dashed to the front door, following the direction of the sounds. "It's across the road and down at old man Jones's place."

They clustered on the dark porch. Flashlights winked in the darkness, and the angry shouts continued. "I can't understand 'em, but at least it's English, so we haven't been invaded by the Japanese," George said in relief. They could hear footsteps hurrying their way.

"Good evening, Mr. Peterson." Jim's voice came through the dark as he walked up the driveway. "Don't worry. There's no danger. Just a drill gone awry."

Alma let her breath out in relief. "What's going on, Jim?"

"That was Bob's first bungled air-raid drill, that's what. Bob forgot to give the all-clear signal because he was so busy running around checking to see that people followed orders." He chuckled. "There he was in his white helmet and whistle, checking every house he could to be sure lights were out and everyone was under a table."

"But what was that ruckus all about?" George asked.

Jim shook his head. "Old man Jones had lights on in his chicken house and wouldn't turn them off. Bob was going to teach him to follow regulations, so he went over there and shot out the lights. A neighbor called me. I had to pull rank and tell Bob to settle down."

"Old man Jones can't be too happy about it," Alma commented.

"He'll be mighty peeved if his hens got so scared they won't lay." Jim sat down on the steps. A peace settled over the evening as the crickets chirped and frogs chorused in the background.

"Trouble is, after that fiasco no one will pay much attention to the next drill," George said. "I'm going back to my paper. Come on, Alma. Sit with me a while." He patted his wife on the back tenderly and opened the screen door.

Jim moved to the porch swing beside Ruth and sighed. "Sometimes you wonder who's the enemy in this," he said dryly. He looked over at her. "How are plans for the Fourth coming? I've been thinking about my speech."

She explained who was involved. "This has been done on short notice, but I think it will turn out okay. People are enthusiastic and willing to help. With gas rationing they'll stay around here for the Fourth, and this will give them something to do."

Jim moved the porch swing with his feet. It added its creak to the chorus of crickets and frogs. "I chose the right person for an assistant even if I did mess up on air-raid warden." He shook his head. "I still can't believe that drill. Bob was supposed to clear it with me, and we'd go over all the details first, but he wanted the authority to do it on his own." He put his hand on hers. "Thanks for all you're doing. I get so busy I don't tell you how much I appreciate you." His look was warm and tender.

Ruth was sure her heart could be heard over nature's chorus. It would be so natural to move closer and put her head on his shoulder. . . *Stop it, Ruth,* she chided herself. She gave a shiver.

"You're getting chilly out here. I'd better let you go in." He stood and helped her to her feet. "Good night, Ruth." He gently touched her nose, turned abruptly, and walked into the dark.

Ruth sat down and moved the swing slowly, enjoying the romantic moment.

twelve

A large banner fluttering between two trees announced the Fourth of July Rally Day. "Over here!" Ruth called out as Marge walked across the school grounds to the grove of fir trees. The Women's Club was busy draping red, white, and blue bunting around the bottom of a raised platform that would serve as a stage. Tables were set up in the shade for the potluck at noon, each decorated with small flags.

"A perfect day," Marge called back as Ruth teetered on a ladder, fastening one end of a banner.

"You're just in time to help, Marge. The girls in the skit will be here any minute. I need you to get them ready." Ruth's mind was on her list of things to do. She climbed down. "The Red Cross is preparing for their demonstration over there. And that's the war bond booth," she explained and pointed.

Joe Duncan drove up in his feed truck. "Where to, Miss Sinclair?"

"Over on the ball field. I'll be right there." She turned. "Come on, Marge. Help me get the trucks ready for the parade." She grabbed several banners and headed for the ball field. "Take the other end, Marge." She held the banner to the side of the truck, and they taped both ends.

"Scrap Metal Drive," Marge read as she stepped back from the decorated truck.

"That's the first one." Ruth surveyed their work, hands on her hips. A small flag fluttered above each fender.

Another truck pulled up and was soon decorated with its banners and flags. Ruth walked back to the feed truck. "Joe, here's the agenda." She handed him a paper. "Just announce each item."

"Miss Sinclair, I. . ."

"You'll do fine, Joe. No one else has a voice loud enough to get people's attention out here."

Joe nodded.

"It's almost time. Let's go." She hurried back to the stage. "You get the girls ready, Marge. I need to find Jim."

Families milled about, talking in small groups and laying out blankets to sit on while children played tag nearby. Ruth searched the crowd. "Jim, there you are," she said in relief as she walked up to him. "I thought you'd skipped out."

"And disappoint a pretty lady? Never! Is everything ready?"

"We'll know in a minute. Here we go." She motioned to Joe, who climbed up on the small stage.

"Attention, please," his voice boomed over the noise of the crowd. "Welcome to our Fourth of July Rally Day. We're here to raise support for our country at war and our men fighting overseas," he read. "Let's open with a prayer by Pastor Cameron."

With the amen, Joe continued. "First on the program is a skit by girls in our school."

Six girls rushed to the stage in red, white, and blue outfits, whispering and giggling. Cynthia Richards gave her recitation flawlessly, followed by the girls' patriotic songs and a short skit. As they finished, the audience clapped and cheered.

"Next we have a first aid demonstration by the Red Cross," Joe announced.

Ruth motioned to Tim, John, and Charlie. They ran to the edge of the stage while the Red Cross director described the first aid classes to be offered at the school. "Now we'll demonstrate some things you'll learn. Boys," he said.

Charlie hopped up on the stage. "Our first boy has a head injury caused by debris from a bomb explosion. We'll demonstrate how to treat it till help arrives." Charlie fell to the ground, clasping his head and moaning. The audience roared with laughter. At this his cries grew louder, and he flopped about the stage. Red ketchup oozed over his forehead, and girls squealed in disgust.

"Lie still, young man. We can't treat you unless you're still," the director hissed. Charlie gave a dramatic flop and lay still while the bandages were applied.

"He's quite the ham," Marge whispered to Ruth.

"It wasn't planned that way," she replied dryly.

Tim and John climbed on the stage as Charlie miraculously recovered. "The next boy was injured in the side and his friend has an arm injury," the director continued.

Tim grabbed his side and with a loud moan fell to the floor. "I'm hit! I'm hit!" he shrieked as the audience doubled over laughing.

John moaned and held his arm, staggering to the side of the stage. He gave his last moan, clutched his arm, and stepped off the edge of the stage. With a cry he tumbled to the ground. "My arm!" he cried. "It really hurts bad!"

"More!" a voice called out.

"Good acting, John!" the crowd shouted.

The director rushed down and helped John to his feet. "My wrist hurts bad, mister." Tears ran down his cheeks. "It hurts so bad. It's not pretend."

The crowd grew silent as the director helped John to the steps while two Red Cross nurses and his mother hurried over.

The director stepped back on stage. "This was not planned, but our nurses will show you how they treat a real sprain. Let's give a big round of applause for our fine actors and a special hand for John." Tim and Charlie jumped up and bowed to the whistles and cheers, and John managed a wave with his good hand.

"After all that excitement you must be hungry. Lunch is waiting," Joe announced. "During the break, be sure to visit the war bond booth and buy some bonds. Kids can meet out on the field for games when they're done eating. We'll continue the program after lunch." The crowd swarmed toward the tables laden with food, then returned to their blankets to enjoy the lunch.

Ruth plopped down with her plate of food. "That was more excitement than we planned. I'll be glad to settle down for a while," she said to Marge.

"May I join you ladies?" Jim asked as he seated himself. "Good crowd. Congratulations to my assistant for a well-organized event. And your actors were superb. I'm not sure the Red Cross appreciated all their antics, but the audience loved them. I checked on John and he'll be fine. A mild sprain."

Ruth took a bite of potato salad. "The boys got carried away, I'm afraid. That wasn't planned." As they ate, Ruth watched families enjoying the day. Shouts and squeals came from the field where children played a game of tag. A soft breeze blew and the sky was clear.

"Ruth, oh, Ruth. Come back, Ruth." Jim waved his hand in front of her face. "No one's allowed to daydream and look so content when I have to worry about being the next speaker." He stood and picked up his plate. "Now, if you'll excuse me, ladies, I need to go over my notes."

"And I need to get the parade lined up." Ruth got to her feet. "Take over, Jim. We'll be waiting for your directions." She hurried to the platform where the musicians were tuning their instruments.

"We're not a large band," Arlan said. "Couldn't get more than two trumpets, a trombone, and the drum. If we play loud, maybe no one will notice."

"You'll do fine," she reassured him.

"Ladies and gentlemen," Joe called out, "we're ready to continue our program. Please be seated." He waited till the crowd was quiet. "Next up is Jim Griffin."

As Jim started his speech, Ruth gave the parade units last-minute instructions.

"The war industry needs our help," Jim continued. "They need materials to make the arms, ammunition, planes, and submarines defending our freedom—freedom to gather as we are today. We can help keep America strong and free!"

A cheer broke out from the crowd.

"Our parade today is the official beginning of Fir Glen's scrap drive. We call it Scraps for Freedom." Jim turned to the band and raised his hand. A drumroll followed, and Wallace Coulter drove Joe's feed truck past the platform with Ruth's "Scrap Metal" banner on the sides and several pieces of scrap metal stacked on the truck. "One shovel will make four hand grenades." Jim held up a shovel, and Tim ran to put it on the truck. "Search your barns and basements. Bring your scrap metal to Bob's lot."

Jim raised his hand again and the drumroll sounded as Bob Miller drove forward, his banners reading "Scrap Rubber Drive." An "Air-Raid Warden" sign had been added below it. "This man wants your old tires, rubber boots, hoses, raincoats—anything rubber. One B-17 bomber requires a half ton of rubber. Keep our men in the air. Bring your scrap rubber to Bob's lot."

Bob honked his horn, leaning out the window, waving and pointing to the "Air-Raid Warden" sign he had added to his door.

At the third drumroll, Velma Miller and Charlotte Hunt marched past the stage carrying a banner between them reading "Grease Collection." In the other hand, each lady held aloft a can of kitchen grease.

Suddenly the truck in front of them gave a loud blast of its horn and jerked to a halt. Bob jumped out and dashed to the back of the truck, grabbing a rubber garden hose that was falling off, one end dragging behind. As he gave a yank, it curled between Velma's feet. With the next jerk, Velma's feet flew out from under her, her grease can sailing through the air.

A collective gasp came from the crowd. "Oh, no!"

"Watch out, Bob!" hollered a bystander as the can headed straight for Bob. With a thud it struck his shoulder. Grease flew into the air and all over Bob.

Joe helped Velma to her feet. She straightened unsteadily, moving her legs carefully as a Red Cross nurse led her away for observation.

The stunned crowd recovered to see their air-raid warden head to toe in grease. A ripple of laughter started in the audience and spread till it became a roar. Men doubled over and slapped their legs. Women laughed so hard they wiped their eyes.

Ruth threw up her hands and hurried over to her grandparents. "Grandpa, would you drive the truck, please? Grandma, will you take Velma's place?" she pleaded. "What'll happen next?"

Bob ran his hands over his greasy, dripping clothes.

"Nice aftershave there, Bob," a voice called out. "That fragrance makes me hungry."

"You won't have to use hair oil for a while," someone else teased.

Bob's face turned an angry red. "After all I've done for Fir Glen, this is the thanks I get." He stomped his feet to shake off a chunk of lard.

"We're only funnin' you, Bob," a man called out.

As Bob stomped off, Joe quickly took the stage. "Let's get back to our program. Jim, it's yours." The crowd quieted.

Jim continued. "Bring your cooking grease in metal containers to Joe's Feed Store."

"Not to Bob!" a voice shouted amid snickers.

"Collection dates will be posted on official bulletin boards. The grease is used to make ammunition." Jim paused.

At the fourth drumroll, Tim and Charlie marched into view, carrying their banner: "Kids, Too!"

"Our young people have been collecting paper and milkweed floss. They'll also be asking for foil from gum and cigarette wrappers," he announced.

Jim looked out over the crowd. "And now to your part. You were asked to bring at least one scrap item to contribute today. The band will lead off, followed by the trucks and marchers. We ask you to place your items on the trucks, join the parade, and march with us to deposit this material at Bob's lot. Then we'll close by singing the national anthem. And as you go, be careful not to slip on the grease."

As the crowd followed Jim's instructions, he came over to Ruth. "Don't look so downhearted. It's a big success."

She shook her head. "First Charlie gets hurt, then Velma falls down, and Bob goes off mad and covered with grease. People won't take this seriously. They'll think it's just a comedy of errors."

"Wrong, Miss Sinclair. You've created a spirit of unity, and they had fun, too. They'll remember what they learned longer than if it had gone perfectly smooth." He took her elbow. "Come on. Let's join them."

The band attempted to play "Stars and Stripes Forever" but quit with a squeak and switched to a simpler tune as the crowd marched to Bob's lot.

"Excuse me a minute, Ruth." Jim hurried over to talk to Joe Duncan. As they reached the lot, Joe raised his hands at the crowd.

"Ladies and gentlemen," his voice boomed, "before we deposit the scraps and sing the closing, we want to thank all who participated. And let's give a special thanks to Miss Sinclair for organizing it all!"

Jim beamed at her as the crowd applauded wildly and cheered.

"Great job, Miss Sinclair!"

"Best Fourth we ever had."

"I'll go home and see what scraps I can bring."

"I'm joining the first aid class this fall."

Comments swirled around Ruth. "Thank you. I appreciate it." She smiled.

"I liked the funny parts. Speeches get boring."

"I'll remember that. I don't think Bob will volunteer again, though," she chuckled.

As the last strains of the anthem faded and people drifted off, Jim grinned at her smugly. "See, I told you."

"Okay, boss, you were right. I don't look forward to my next trip to Bob's market, though," she said with a grin. "But it seems to be successful in spite of everything. I'm so tired, but in a good way."

"Let's go see about the cleanup. Then you deserve a ride home." Jim took her arm and led her toward the school. The cleanup crew was busy returning tables to the school building and dismantling the decorations when Jim and Ruth got to the grove and joined the effort.

Ruth picked up the last scrap of paper. "That's it. I'm ready for that ride you offered."

"Car's over here." Jim led the way, carrying the box of supplies Ruth had brought. She climbed in with a sigh and laid her head back on the seat. Jim chuckled. "Looks like we wore out my assistant today."

He pulled into the Peterson driveway and turned to her. "I appreciate all you did, Ruth." He reached for her hand. "We make a good team." He looked down. "I'm sorry it has such limitations." He looked at her tenderly but sadly and said softly, "But I respect your stand. Good night, Ruth—and thanks again."

thirteen

The morning sun shone through the bedroom window, giving the room a golden glow as the rays danced on the flowered wallpaper. Ruth stretched and lay back, listening to the birds warbling in the tree outside her window.

"The Lord must love mornings. He made them so beautiful," she said aloud. She swung her legs over the edge of the bed. "Lord, thank You for a safe new day." She completed her morning devotions, dressed, and went downstairs.

"Good morning, sleepyhead," Alma teased as she folded the clothes she'd brought in from the clothesline. "I got up early to get these done before it gets hot."

Ruth poured a cup of coffee. "All the summer's activity finally got to me, I guess, Grandma. You shouldn't let me sleep so long."

Alma folded the last towel and added it to the pile. "Do you feel like a trip to town today? Emerson's Grocery in Brookwood has a sale on. We need coffee and a few essentials."

Ruth nodded. "What time?"

"In about an hour, I need to check my grocery list against my ration books and the ads to see what I can buy."

"I'll be upstairs cleaning. Call me when you're ready, Gram."

≥∝

An hour later, Ruth turned into the parking lot beside the grocery store. "Here we are, Grandma. Ready for the big adventure?"

Alma sighed and picked up her pocketbook. "I don't look forward to this. Shopping is so hard with the shortages and ration stamps. I'm just thankful we can grow so much of our own food."

They entered the market and wandered down the aisles,

looking for specials. Out of curiosity, Alma picked up a can of applesauce. "Can you believe it? Sixteen cents! When we get home, I'm going out to sweet-talk our apple trees!"

Ruth chuckled. "I'm sure you will, Grandma."

Alma peered at the meat display. "Hamburger—forty-three cents a pound. Grandpa's butchering soon. We'll wait." She walked on. "We need to check on Maxwell House coffee. They may have a good special to celebrate their fifty years on the market. Let's head for that aisle. And keep your eye out for sugar. I need to use my stamps before the end of the month, but there hasn't been any in stock."

With several items in the basket, Alma stopped to check her purchases and her ration books. "I'm too old for this, Ruth. Let's go." Alma reached the cashier and counted out the required ration stamps and money. "Grocery trips wear me out these days," she sighed as they headed for the car.

"You get in and sit down. I'll load the groceries," Ruth directed. She could feel the day's heat bearing down.

She put the last of the purchases in the trunk. As she looked up, she saw Jim coming out of the county clerk's office across the street. Her heart gave its usual extra thump. Then she looked again. Someone was with him. A blond woman. Young and very pretty. The woman smiled up at Jim as she talked.

Ruth slammed the trunk lid and climbed into the car. *That odd feeling can't be jealousy,* she chided herself. She started the car and was turning around when Alma exclaimed, "There's Jim Griffin. Say, who's that woman with him?"

"Probably someone from the county clerk's office. As community coordinator he works with various government departments," Ruth responded casually, making a strong effort not to betray her feelings.

"That doesn't look like business to me. She's holding his arm. Oh, dear, I was hoping you'd become interested in Mr. Griffin. He's such a fine Christian man."

"You never cared for Harold, did you, Grandma?"

Alma hesitated. "I never disliked him. I just didn't feel he was a sincere Christian or very settled. I wanted only the best for you."

"I know, Gram. When Harold comes home, that's something I have to settle."

"Don't wait too long, dear. Mr. Griffin's an attractive man. He won't wait forever. There's that woman. . ."

Ruth laughed. "You're impossible." *But right,* she thought. *I never expected Jim to find someone else before Harold came home.* An uneasy feeling crept into her heart. She backed out of the parking space and took one more look toward the county clerk's office, but Jim and the woman were nowhere in sight. With a sigh, she pulled out of the parking lot and headed home.

Ruth turned into their driveway and pulled up by the back door.

"Let's get these groceries put away. This heat isn't good for them or me," Alma said as she got out of the car.

"I'll do it," Ruth insisted. "You go inside."

Alma sighed. "In this heat you don't have to push much. Shopping and heat wear me out." She paused at the round bed of zinnias and marigolds ablaze in blossoms of yellow and orange, red and purple. The flowers drooped in the day's heat. "I have to get these watered today, too. Don't let me forget, Ruth." She headed for the house. "I'm glad Oregon doesn't have a whole summer like this."

Ruth set the groceries on the counter and paused to fix her grandmother some cold juice. "Take this and go sit in the living room. You rest while I get all this put away. That's an order."

Alma patted Ruth's shoulder. "Thank you, dear. You're good to me." She took her cold drink and walked to the living room.

"You deserve it," Ruth called after her. She turned to put the groceries away.

"Ruth! Oh, no, Ruth, come here. What's happened?" Alma called out.

Ruth's heart gave a lurch. "Lord, let her be okay," she whispered as she rushed to the living room with a sinking feeling. "Are you all right, Grand—" Ruth stopped and stared at the mess as she entered the room.

"Look at this," Alma whispered. Books were torn out of the bookcase and scattered over the floor. George's desk was a mess of strewn papers. "Someone was in our house while we were gone." Alma sat down heavily. "What could they want? We don't keep money here." She stared at the mess and shook her head. "Grandpa's working with some of the men out in Nakamuras' field. We can't get ahold of him. Oh, my, what do we do, Ruth?"

"I don't know," Ruth replied, "but I'm calling Jim. This is the third bookcase ransacked—and someone got in our house."

Jim arrived ten minutes later.

"The same thing happened at school and the Nakamuras'," she explained. "What does someone want?"

"Have you seen anyone suspicious around here?" he asked.

Both women shook their heads. "And nothing's been taken that we can see. It's just a big mess," Ruth replied.

Jim looked among the books. "When you clean up, check carefully to be sure nothing's missing. I'll tell the sheriff, but as I said before, he wasn't very concerned about the two previous incidents. With a war on, he's got other things to worry about, he says."

"What bothers me is that someone was in our house," Alma said softly.

He was quiet and looked concerned. "I don't like it, either, even if these are pranks, as the sheriff seems to think. Maybe someone's still upset about your friendship with the Nakamuras. Anti-Japanese sentiment is strong in some people." He looked sharply at Ruth. "Don't take any chances. Be sure to lock your doors. Let me know if anything else happens, however small."

Alma shook her head sadly. "What's the world coming to when we distrust others and have to lock our doors? I never thought I'd see the day."

Jim picked up his hat. "I'll speak to the sheriff, but since I've been here, I'm sure he won't send someone out." He looked at Ruth soberly. "Be careful." He turned to Alma. "Don't worry, Mrs. Peterson. I'll see what I can do about it." He smiled at Ruth and was gone.

"We're blessed compared to people in Europe, but I still feel invaded when someone has been in our home." Alma sighed, sat back in her chair, and fanned herself with a paper.

"Drink your juice and rest. I'll get all this cleaned up. Grandpa can check his desk," Ruth said as she began to put the books back.

"I think I'll lie down a bit." Alma got up and walked to the hall. "The war seems closer today—all the ration stamps and now this. After lunch I want to work on the banner for our window. We're proud Bud's in the service defending our country." She paused. "And we're blessed we can put up a blue star for Bud. On the way home today, I saw a banner with one gold star and two blue. Can you imagine—three men in that family in the service and now one killed or missing in action. We need to talk with the Lord a lot, Ruth." She turned toward her room.

Ruth plopped down on the sofa, trying to sort out her thoughts. *Someone was in our home!* She paused as she thought of the scene in their living room and Jim's quick effort to help. *I've come to rely on him a lot,* she admitted. Finally with a sigh she got up and walked to the kitchen. *This won't get the work done or solve the problem.*

She had put the last of the groceries away and tidied the room when Alma walked in. "You were supposed to rest," she chided her grandmother.

"I'm better now, dear. When I've had a talk with the Lord, I'm rested." She got out the material and started on the banner for their window. Ruth joined her as she measured and cut the material. "It's looking good," Alma commented later, "but I need to stop and knit awhile, Ruth. The Ladies Aid wants to ship our batch of socks overseas soon, and I'm behind on what I promised to make." She folded the material and straightened up. "Knitting's a quiet thing to do on a hot day."

"Good. It'll make you sit still and rest awhile, too," Ruth said with satisfaction as she got up. "I'm going for a walk in the woods, Gram. Will you be okay here by yourself? I need to think."

"No one will bother me, dear. Those hoodlums only come when nobody's home. Run along, but be careful for poison oak."

Ruth walked across the yard and headed for the woods behind the barn. A narrow path left the pasture and wound into the trees. The warm air was fragrant with the smell of fir needles, and insects buzzed as she wandered down the path. Oregon grape brushed against her legs.

She came to a moss-covered log and sat down. *My thinking spot,* she remembered as she looked about the small clearing covered by a canopy of leaves. *I've come here so many times over the summers.* A breeze lazily moved the vine maple leaves above her.

When I was little, I pretended this was my house, and the moss was my carpet. It was all safe and secure and special. I even imagined my dolls could come to life here. I miss that innocent world. Anything was possible, and everything was exciting.

A fly buzzed about her head. She swatted at it. *But the world's not like that. An innocent world is the one that's pretend. Even here there are bugs to bite you and plants to make you itch.* She turned at a rustling in the underbrush. *It's that way out there, too. But I want to nestle into a world where everything's good and safe and happy. I don't like it when evils and troubles intrude.* The fly buzzed around her again. She gave a sigh. *They've intruded in a big way this time.*

She sat on the log swinging her legs. *I'd like to return to Eden, but I can't. There's sin in this world, and all our efforts and longings won't make it perfect. Only God can do that.*

The woods responded with chirps and buzzes and the soft breeze rustling the leaves. A squirrel stopped in its run up a tree and chattered at her intrusion into its world.

She stood and dusted off her slacks. *Well, now Jim's a worry, too. Has he found someone else?*

A spider made its way along an almost-invisible strand of web. She ducked and started on the path back to the house with a sigh. *And I never dreamed I'd be harassed because of a friendship either, but that's what's happening. We're being threatened because we won't desert our Japanese friends.* She stepped over an old log and moved a small branch out of the way with her hand.

Helpless, that's how I feel. Jim said I had to grow out of my greenhouse faith. Is that what this is all about, Lord? Are You trying to teach me to have faith when life's hard and out of control as well as when it's good? A long, briered vine tugged at her pant leg, and she stooped to release her slacks from the sharp thorns.

She left the woods and walked through the pasture in the late afternoon sun. The cows rested in the shade, and ahead Fluffy was stretched out on the porch. "Your world looks peaceful today, Fluffy," she said to the cat as she climbed the steps and reached to open the screen door. "Mine's not so peaceful. I have two new worries. Who broke in our house? And is Jim giving up on me?"

fourteen

Ruth climbed the wooden steps of the old feed store and breathed deeply. *Mm, the smell of hay and feed is pleasant,* she thought. *It reminds me of the fun Bud and I had playing in Grandpa's barn when we were kids.*

"Hi, Joe." She smiled at the owner as he unloaded sacks of grain from a truck. He raised his hand in greeting. "I'll need five sacks of chicken feed before I leave today. I brought Grandpa's pickup."

"Sure thing, Miss Sinclair." He put the sack down on the pile. "You can have your grease collection over there." He pointed to the end of the long wooden loading dock where two metal barrels were located.

"Thanks. I'll put my poster up on the wall behind them, if that's okay."

Joe nodded.

She walked to the end of the dock and inspected the poster she had lettered: "Grease collection here. Save waste fats for ammunition!" She held the poster to the wall and fumbled in her purse. "Oh, no, I forgot the thumbtacks." She lowered the sign. "Joe," she called, "I'm going over to Bob's store. I'll be right back." She grabbed her purse and hurried across the road.

The bell jangled above the door as she entered the market where Bob was on a ladder putting up a Royal Crown Cola poster. "I'm looking for thumbtacks, Bob."

"Can't get 'em now," he replied. "War shortages, you know. You'll have to use tape. It's down that aisle and on the left." He climbed down the ladder and stood with his thumbs hooked in his suspenders. "I guess you heard the news." He looked around to be sure no one else was there and lowered his voice. "A shipment from Griffin's factory was broken into." He nodded his head smugly.

"Who did it?" Ruth was shocked.

"Spies, that's what. Found out about the shipment and broke into it. Has to do with lights people see around the plant."

"This is terrible!"

Bob nodded eagerly. "Those Nazis have been sinkin' our ships off the East Coast. I say spies are signaling 'em our ships' locations. If they're doing it on the East Coast, you can bet we got spies out here, too." He pursed his lips and rocked up on his toes.

Ruth tried to grasp what she was hearing. "How could they do that without being noticed?"

"Plow signals in the fields. Bonfires. Them little lights. They're clever. Got to keep your eyes open. Keeps me busy checking on everyone."

Ruth shuddered. "I have to run, Bob. Grease collection at the feed store." She paid for her purchase. "Thanks."

No wonder I haven't seen much of Jim lately, Ruth thought as she hurried back to the feed store. She arrived to find two members of the Fir Glen Women's Club waiting.

"I had to go over to Bob's for tape." She put her purse down on a feed sack next to her notebook and *Ben-Hur.* "Mrs. Olson, if you'll hold that end of the poster, I'll get it taped up."

She applied the tape and stood back to survey their work. "Okay, ladies, we're all set. To our posts. Actually, to our barrels," Ruth quipped with a smile.

The women glanced at each other. "You look, uh, comfortable, dear, in those slacks. I would never wear them myself, of course, but I suppose they are handy in some circumstances, though for a teacher in public. . ." Mrs. Archer stood primly in her well-cut suit and matching hat, carrying white gloves.

Ruth's face grew red. "This can be a messy job scraping grease out of cans and buckets. No use splattering good clothes."

"To each her own," Mrs. Olson snipped. "I intend to keep records for this collection, so I dressed appropriately for that." She turned to her fellow clubwoman, similarly dressed. "Mrs. Archer, you see that everyone stays in line and give them directions. This must remain orderly," she directed. "You never know what kind of people will be here."

Ruth felt her anger rise. "Then who will man the second barrel?"

The women looked at each other. "If you didn't think to arrange for someone, I guess you will have to do both, dear."

"But that's why you're here," Ruth protested.

"Dear, you can't expect us to scrape grease out of cans into a barrel. If it splatters, our clothes will be ruined. We have bridge club later."

"That's why I wore. . ." She stopped. *Okay, Ruth,* she told herself, *admit it. You've been had.*

"I hear our first contributors coming now," Mrs. Olson said briskly. "Mrs. Archer, you direct them to me. I'll record who they are and how much they brought, then send them on to Miss Sinclair."

A line of children and a few adults soon formed, each carrying a metal container of lard or grease. Ruth poured what she could into the barrel and scraped out the more solid form. The line seemed endless, and the smell of bacon grease grew nauseating in the summer heat.

"This looks exciting." Ruth looked up to see Jim watching her. He glanced around. "Why are you the only one at this end of the line? Those ladies don't seem to be doing much."

"Because I'm a chump. I dressed for it. They cleverly didn't. At this rate we'll be here all day."

Jim took off his suit coat and rolled up his shirtsleeves. "Your hero to the rescue, ma'am."

"Jim, you can't. You're dressed up," Ruth protested as he winked at her.

"Do you think I'd leave a lovely damsel in distress?"

"Oh, Mr. Griffin." Mrs. Olson bustled over. "You shouldn't

be doing that; you, the community coordinator, and in your good clothes."

"We do what we can to help out, Mrs. Olson," he said evenly. "No job is too small or too messy. Miss Sinclair needed help, and there didn't seem to be anyone else willing, so I volunteered."

"Well, I—we—didn't expect, I mean. . ." she sputtered, turned briskly, and walked back to her records.

"Next time, I'll request help willing to dress for the part and work where needed," Ruth said wryly.

"After this we should send them over to Bob's to sort messy, empty toothpaste tubes," Jim chuckled as they waited for the next contributor.

Ruth smiled. "I haven't seen you around. Things busy lately?"

"Problems at the plant. You know how business goes," he replied evasively. "I have such an able assistant; she carries on when I'm otherwise occupied."

"Half an hour to go. Our line's thinning out," Ruth observed. "I won't be sorry when this is over."

"Oh, Mr. Griffin." Mrs. Olson hurried over. "Our women's club would like to have you as guest speaker at our next meeting." She smiled sweetly. "We'd be honored to have you speak on the war effort."

Jim glanced at Ruth and sighed. "To help the war effort, what can I say? Let me know the time and place, Mrs. Olson."

"I'll have my daughter get in touch with you. She's a secretary in the Brookwood mayor's office, you know. Being single, she has more time than I do. She'd be here today, but she's working." Mrs. Olson smiled proudly.

"Fine. And, thank you, ladies, for your help. We've taken up too much of your time. I'm sure you have things to do." He ushered them to the steps and smiled. With a wave of their white-gloved hands, they were gone.

"Well, Mr. Griffin, Fir Glen's society has its eye on you for its daughters. Do you like teas?" Ruth teased.

Jim grimaced. "Spare me, please." He looked around. "Is there much left to do?"

Ruth shook her head. "The truck will be here to pick up the barrels any minute. I think it went well." She turned to a pile of grain sacks, picked up her notebook, and hunted around.

"Missing something?"

"My purse. I left it here with my notebook. Now it's gone." She looked behind the sacks. "*Ben-Hur's* missing, too."

"I'll check down here," Jim said as he searched the length of the loading dock. "Nothing there."

"I left them with my notebook. Nothing's ever stolen in Fir Glen."

"You seem to attract the strangest problems, Miss Sinclair. Ransacked bookcases are one thing, but a stolen purse is a matter for the sheriff. I'll make a call and be right back." He turned toward the feed store office.

"Miss Sinclair, are you still here?" a voice called from the end of the dock.

Jim stopped. "She's at the other end. Come on up."

Cynthia Richards approached and held out a brown purse. "Is this yours? I found it around the corner by some bushes. The stuff was scattered all over the ground. I put it back in."

Ruth took the purse. "Yes, it's mine. Thank you, Cynthia. I was looking all over for it." Ruth let out her breath in relief.

Cynthia beamed. "Well, gotta go. Glad you have it back."

Ruth poured out the contents and reorganized the items. "That's odd, Jim. Nothing's missing."

"You're sure?"

"Positive. These incidents have to be pranks. Otherwise, something would be missing—other than *Ben-Hur,* that is. I feel so bad about Suzi's book. This is a message aimed at me because of my friendship with the Nakamuras. Loud and clear it says, 'Don't befriend any Japanese.' Remember the man who hollered at me last spring when I fell in the mud? That was my warning!"

Jim stared at the purse. "Keep your eyes open, Ruth, for

anyone suspicious." He stood, reached down, and lifted her chin with his finger. "Stay safe. I'm late for an appointment. Can you finish up on your own?"

Ruth nodded and he hurried away.

She sat down on a feed sack, catching her breath. *That man can leave me breathless and limp as a cooked noodle,* she admitted to herself. *Why do my head and heart have to pull in opposite directions?*

❧

An hour later, Ruth arrived home and climbed her porch steps with a sigh. "That was a long, hot day," she said aloud and opened the back door. As she put her notebook down on the table, an envelope caught her eye. "A letter from Harold! It's been so long."

She took a deep breath. "You won't find out what it says by staring at it, Ruth Sinclair." She picked it up and went into the living room. "Opened by Censor" was stamped across the front. "Oh," she grimaced, "that means the censor will have cut out half of it, and it won't make sense."

She sat down and took out the paper. "I'm nervous," she said out loud. "If he's coming home soon, I'll have to face some hard discussions."

"Dear Ruth," she read, "I'm. . .after two weeks. . ." *This is irritating. Is he coming home in two weeks? I don't know what he's saying.* She continued the letter. "We've been friends for a long time now. I wanted you to be the first to hear my good news. By the time you read this I'll be married. . . ."

Ruth's hand dropped to her lap. A jolt of shock went through her, and her mind couldn't grasp what she had read. She slowly picked up the letter and read the words again. "By the time you read this I'll be married. She's a wonderful girl. You'll love her. She works in. . . We've been dating awhile and with life so. . .we decided, why not? When I get home, I'll come by and introduce her. I know you'll be good friends. Got to go. Take care. Always, Harold."

She sat back in the chair trying to get her breath. *I feel as if the wind's been knocked out of me,* she thought. *Harold married!* "We've been friends for a long time." A wave of anger swept over her. "I worried about breaking up, when to him we were only friends. How could I have been so stupid?"

She looked at the letter. "We've been dating awhile. . ." All the dates she'd turned down with Jim to be loyal, and Harold was dating someone else—and seriously. She threw the letter down and got up. "I'm supposed to be crying my eyes out, but I'm too mad," she fumed.

The phone rang three times before she recognized the sound and picked it up. "Hello. . .hi, Marge. . . Do I know a young blond woman—pretty—tall? I don't think so, why. . .? She and Jim ate at the café and left together? Probably business. . . No, you'd think any close, personal conversation was romantic, Marge. I. . ." Ruth's anger melted as she remembered the woman she had seen with Jim in Brookwood, and she suddenly found herself crying.

The phone slipped from her ear and dropped toward the floor, bouncing at the end of its cord as Ruth covered her face with her hands and sobbed.

"Ruth, what's the matter? I didn't mean to upset you. Ruth. . . Ruth. . . Oh, my, I'll be right over. Stay there." Marge's voice could be heard from the dangling receiver. The phone clicked. Ruth stood there listening to the buzz as she wiped at her wet face.

She finally put the receiver back on the hook and sat down in the chair, trying to piece together what was happening. How could the world fall apart so completely in a couple of hours? She jumped up as loud pounding sounded at the door, and she opened it quickly to see Marge with her fist raised to pound again.

"Are you trying to punch me in the face, Marge? Come on in. I've already had all the punches I can take for one day."

"What's going on, Ruth? You're white as a sheet." Marge frowned with concern as she hurried in and stared at her friend.

"You'd better sit down." Ruth led her to the living room couch. "Read this. It came in the mail today." She handed Marge Harold's letter and leaned back as Marge read.

She looked up at Ruth quickly. "He's married? I don't believe it! Is this a joke?"

"Read on, Marge."

"Just friends? He's going to bring her by? And you've been sitting here turning down dates with Jim Griffin and. . ." Her face registered her sudden awareness of what she had said earlier on the phone. "Oh, Ruth, I'm so sorry. Me and my big mouth. Jim and that woman probably just had some business to discuss." Marge stopped, not knowing what to say next.

"I've seen them together myself, Marge. After my big mistake in judgment with Harold, I don't think Jim was ever interested in me. He's just a flirt and I fell for it. Get that look off your face, Marge. Yes, I admit it. Like a fool, I fell for Jim Griffin."

Marge nodded. "I knew it, but I sure don't feel any satisfaction in an 'I told you so' now." She shook her head in disbelief. "This is my first failure as a matchmaker."

The room became quiet, and the clock ticked louder and louder. "Will you be okay, Ruth? I need to go."

"Run on home, Marge. I'm so mad at my stupidity, but I'll be okay. I need some time to think before Grandma and Grandpa come back anyway. Thanks for being here for me."

The screen door slammed, and Ruth began to pace the floor in silence. "Lord," she said finally, "I know this seems small compared to what people in the rest of the world have to suffer from the war, but it still hurts—badly. This could have been an answer to my confusion, but I waited too long, and Jim found someone else. What do I do now? How do I work with him? At least he doesn't know the latest about Harold or my feelings, so maybe we can go on without embarrassment."

She sat down and put her face in her hands. "Please help me, Lord. I feel so alone tonight."

fifteen

The next morning Ruth sat across the kitchen table from her grandmother, as they drank their morning coffee. "We got home late last night, dear. Your light was out. We didn't want to disturb you." Alma took a sip of the coffee. "Grandpa helped the Ericksons with their wheat harvest, and I went along to help Cora with the cooking. Everyone got to talking, too, so it took longer than we figured."

Ruth sat quietly with her hands around the cup. Alma looked at her sharply. "Did you get your letter?"

Ruth nodded.

"I guess it wasn't good news," Alma ventured.

"It makes me feel like a fool." She reached into her pocket, pulled out Harold's letter, and handed it to Alma.

Her grandmother put her cup down and adjusted her glasses as she began to read. "Oh, my, I can't believe it!" Alma exclaimed as she looked up from the letter.

"I know what you just read, Gram. Read the rest."

Alma finished the letter and shook her head. "I'm not pleased with something that hurts you, Ruth."

"And that's not all. Jim's seeing another woman. The one we saw him with in Brookwood. I took so long, he gave up— if he really was interested. If I could be so wrong about Harold, I was probably wrong there, too."

"No, dear, I. . ."

"I feel like such a fool, Grandma. Twice. I was just starting to admit I cared for Jim. I never thought I'd end up an old-maid schoolteacher."

"That's taking this a bit far, Ruth. You're young. God knows who's right for you. Take this to Him and let Him handle it."

Ruth pushed her chair back and glanced at the clock. "At least I have plenty to keep me busy. I meet with the Junior Volunteers this morning at the school." She wiped her forehead. "My, it's warm already."

Alma agreed. "It'll be another scorcher. August never goes by fast enough for me. This heat'll bring on the beans again, too. Canning is so hard in the heat."

"You rest today, Grandma. I'll pick the beans early tomorrow morning, and we'll try to get them done before it gets hot." She picked up her notebook. "At least in Oregon we don't have too much of this heat. Grandpa says the rains always start with Labor Day. Cooler weather will be here soon. And so will school," she added. "While I'm at the school, I'll stop by my classroom. Staying busy will be good for me right now."

"I feel too old to be much help at a time like this, Ruth." Alma patted Ruth's arm and fanned herself with a paper. "Talk to your mother about it next time she calls. She'll know what to say."

"You've been wonderful, Grandma. You keep me focused on the Lord and remind me He's in control. That's what I need." She gave Alma a hug. "I won't be long."

Ruth hurried to the school yard to find a group of children waiting under the shade of a tree. "Hey, Miss Sinclair, you're late! It's five minutes after ten." Tim was gleeful. "Miss Sinclair is tardy," he chanted.

Cynthia began to imitate Tim. "Hey, Miss Sinclair," she taunted. "Hay, hay, hay. Straw is cheaper; grass is free, Tim Henderson."

"What do you know? You're a girl," Tim retorted.

"Okay, kids, that's enough. We have work to do," Ruth reminded them.

The children sat down on the grass. Charlie yanked the back of Carrie's hair. She started to yelp, but a look from Ruth quieted them.

"You've done very well this summer collecting paper and foil. Oh, yes, and milkweed floss," she complimented. "Now we need your legs and your bikes."

Eyes grew big. "You need our what, Miss Sinclair?" Tim squeaked. Sunday's paper had featured a soldier who had lost a leg in the war.

Ruth burst out laughing, realizing what she'd said and how they'd taken it. "No, not to put in the scrap drive," she said as she looked at their horrified faces. "I mean we need them to go collecting. People have metal and rubber junk in their basements, barns, and attics they could contribute to the scrap drive. We need you to go door-to-door and ask people to give all they can. If they can't get the scraps to Bob's lot, a truck will come by to pick them up. Can you do that?"

Heads nodded enthusiastically.

"We need to get this done before school starts. Tim will be captain again for the next school year. We'll use the same organization as last time so we won't miss any houses. I'll go by the places that are too far for you to reach on your bikes. That's all I have for now."

As the group wandered off, Tim and Charlie walked with Ruth toward her classroom. "Me and Charlie told Mr. Griffin about the lights around his plant. We've been checking on spies all summer," Tim informed her. Charlie nodded. "And we're checking the lights at Billy Nakamura's, too. Me and Charlie and Billy used to play in the creek by their place. Me and Charlie were down there last week and saw the lights there, too."

"What are you doing down there at night?" Ruth asked as they stopped outside the building.

"I have to pick beans all day. We're building a raft after I get home. And we saw old man Jones snooping around there, too. Mr. Miller says we need to keep an eye on him. He's susticious," Tim declared.

"Suspicious, Tim," she corrected. "You boys be careful. Let Mr. Griffin and the officials know. This doesn't sound like something for two boys to handle."

"We will. Bye, Miss Sinclair. We gotta go get our aluminum

so we can get in the movies to see Roy Rogers. It's an aluminum matinee. Charlie doesn't have any money. If we take aluminum to give 'em, we get in free. See ya."

Ruth smiled at the two and let herself into the school building. She paused and looked around. *Maybe this will be my life—school, teaching, kids. Could I be happy with only this? Do I have a choice?*

She opened her classroom and stepped in. "I'll take home last year's plan book and my teacher's manuals," she murmured. "And these." She picked up two books. "I'll have to plan special work for Tim in English and spelling."

As she added the books to the pile, a strip of light cardboard floated to the floor. She reached down. "Suzi's bookmark! I wondered where it went." Suzi's beautiful drawings of flowers and birds covered the edges of the paper, with angels in the center. "Now if I had her copy of *Ben-Hur,* I'd feel more comfortable." She tucked the slip in the material for Tim and locked the door.

The sun's rays were hot as she crossed the school yard and headed for the road. "The traffic gets busier by the year," she observed while she waited for cars to pass. She noticed two people come out of Bob's market across the road, then looked again. "That looks like Jim—and the woman." She watched as they walked to Jim's car, laughing and chatting easily.

Ruth sized up the woman. *Pretty. Blond. Tall and slim. Stylish. Looks outgoing and very confident.* She sighed. "Well, that's that. I can't compete with her. I'll put Jim Griffin behind me and get on with life. I'm glad I wasn't too head over heels before I found out."

The traffic cleared and she crossed the road, watching Jim's car disappear.

❧

"How was your meeting?" Alma inquired when Ruth got home. She was rolling out a piecrust. Flour and ingredients were spread over the table, and Alma had a white dab of flour on the end of her nose.

"Great. The Junior Volunteers work hard," she replied. She carried her books to the stairs as the phone rang, and she picked it up to Marge's hello. "Shopping. . .? I guess so. I do need to buy some things before school starts. . . . I'll meet you at the bus stop at nine." She hung up and walked over to Alma.

"Marge and I are going shopping in Portland Saturday. There's time to do some sewing before school starts if I get the material now. And this will keep me too busy to pine away."

❧

Sunday morning Ruth was adjusting her new hat in the hall mirror as Alma came out of her room dressed for church. "That hat looks lovely, dear, but how did you resist the fancy ones with all the fruit and feathers piled on top?"

"Easy, Grandma. You wouldn't believe the prices. So I settled for a plain and practical navy with a ribbon around it. I do like the wider brim, though."

"That'll be good for gardening. And birds won't be trying to eat it or make a nest in the feathers," George commented as he came down the hall in his Sunday suit.

"Grandpa, where's your sense of fashion?" Ruth teased as she carefully thrust the hatpin into the hat.

"Makes no sense to me. You don't wear your food on your head or put feathers up there if you don't want birds making a nest in 'em."

Alma took her husband by the elbow. "Go on, George, get the car or we'll be late for church. What women wear makes no less sense than that piece of cloth you men wear around your necks and call a tie." Alma winked at Ruth as George went out the door.

On the way to church, Ruth wondered if Jim would bring the woman to the service. As they pulled into the parking lot, she scanned the groups of people. *I just don't want to be caught off guard,* she thought.

The three entered the sanctuary and sat down in a pew. Ruth settled back, then turned as a movement in the aisle caught her eye. She looked up to see Jim escorting his parents—and the woman—to a front pew. *Why do I keep being surprised and hurt?* she thought. She joined in the singing but soon found herself staring into space, seeing the woman holding Jim's arm. She gave her head a shake and prayed. *Lord, help me clear my thoughts. I'm in a turmoil.* When she looked up, Pastor Cameron was closing his Bible and announcing the closing hymn.

The congregation rose to leave. "Miss Sinclair." Tim Henderson's mother came up behind Ruth as she tried to edge through the crowd before the Griffins made their way past her.

Trapped, she thought and turned.

"Tim will be in your sixth grade this year. I know he struggles in English and spelling. If he can have some extra work, I'll see that he gets it done." Mrs. Henderson spoke earnestly.

Ruth nodded. "Good, Mrs. Henderson. I'm working on special lessons for him now. If we keep in close touch, I think we can help him out this year."

Mrs. Henderson agreed and moved away. As Ruth waited for the crowd to disperse ahead of her, she heard the familiar voice that made her heart race.

"You need to ask Miss Sinclair about that, Stan," she overheard Jim saying to Stan Evans.

"Aw, please, Mr. Griffin. Miss Sinclair just got dumped. She won't want to," Stan wheedled.

She could hear Jim pause before he asked, "What do you mean, she got dumped?"

"That guy Harold she wrote to. He up and married some lady in England. I heard my sister Marge talking about it. He sent her a letter or something," Stan explained. "Please, Mr. Griffin."

"I'll let you know, Stan."

Ruth could feel the rush of embarrassment flowing over her. She looked quickly for an escape, but Jim had seen her and made his way toward her. The woman stood chatting with his parents.

She put on a smile and chattered quickly, "Hi, boss. The Junior Volunteers are organized to canvass the neighborhood before school starts."

"Good, good." He didn't return her smile. Instead, he handed her a paper. "I need this typed and posted by tomorrow. Sorry it's such a rush, but it's very important it be up as soon as possible."

She took the paper and looked at it. "No problem. I can get it done."

He looked down a moment and then closely at her. "Ruth, life's not always what it seems. I. . ." He appeared uncomfortable. "I can't say more, but just remember that. Please." His eyes pleaded with her. "I've got to go. Thanks for your help."

At least he's uncomfortable for being such a flirt and leading me on, Ruth thought. *Life sure wasn't what it seemed around him. Maybe he was seeing this woman all along, and I was just a diversion. How could I be so dumb?* She looked down at the paper. *In this small community I can't avoid him. I can't quit the war work. It's too important.*

She walked out the door and toward the car, where her grandparents waited. *Just push it all away, Ruth, and grow up, just as you tell your students to do when they have a hopeless crush on someone.*

sixteen

Pattern pieces and brown gabardine material were scattered across the dining room floor. Ruth crouched, pinning patterns, her lips holding the pins.

"That will make a sensible skirt for school," Alma commented as she came into the room. "Will you get it done for the first day of class?"

"Umm, uh um," Ruth mumbled through the pins. She sat back and took the pins from her lips. "Sorry, Gram. I hope so. I'll have a good outfit for fall when I get the blouse made, too. And it'll stay in style longer than the new military look that's coming out."

"One thing about getting old. You worry less about clothes. A few housedresses, a nice navy, and a flowered dress for good, and lots of big aprons. That does me just fine," Alma declared.

Ruth folded her material and patterns. "We have our first teachers' meeting at 11:00 this morning. Planning the school year and dividing up duties. Then some time in our rooms getting ready for the first day." She put her sewing away. "The summer certainly flew." *Thankfully, the next weeks will be too busy to worry about Jim Griffin,* she thought. *I'm safe except for the Friday night Bible study Jim's starting. I'm sorry now I promised to help out.*

❧

The four teachers gathered around the table in Mrs. Hastings' room, discussing schedules of recess duty, music, and lunch hour. "Ruth, would you inventory the playground equipment? With a war on we'll have to repair and make do."

Ruth nodded as a sharp rap sounded at the door. Mrs. Hastings hurried to open it. "Come in, Mr. Griffin. We're at a good place for a break."

Ruth shifted uncomfortably in her chair. *Just what I needed today—facing Jim Griffin!*

Mrs. Hastings turned to the group. "Ladies, Mr. Griffin has asked to brief us on civilian defense policies that concern the school. Please take notes so we'll make no mistakes in procedures."

Jim took a seat at the table and smiled at the teachers, his gaze lingering on Ruth. Her heart gave the familiar nervous thump.

"I want to discuss monthly air raid drills and the procedures to use," he began. As he went through the steps, Ruth's mind flitted back and forth between what he said and how good he looked dressed in his dark brown business suit.

I'm just like the kids, she thought. *What I can't have is the most appealing.* "During air-raid drills, practice getting the children to the basement as quickly as possible," he stressed as he finished his presentation. "Their safety depends on it."

"Thank you for coming, Mr. Griffin," Mrs. Hastings concluded. "Ladies, we'll break for lunch and come back to finish up at 1:00."

Jim stayed at the table when the teachers rose to leave the room. "Ruth, may I see you a moment?" He was quiet and sat looking at the papers in front of him. "I have a few things to be typed." He seemed uncomfortable instead of the flirting, teasing Jim she was used to.

"What do you have for me to do?" she finally asked.

He looked up and stared at her a moment. "Type these two, if you would. And mail them as soon as possible." He looked down and fingered the papers. "Ruth, I. . .uh, I. . ."

She couldn't stand the tension and his obvious discomfort around her. She picked up the papers. "No problem. I'll get them done right away. Please excuse me, Jim. I have some things to do before we meet again at one." She turned away abruptly as Jim said a soft thanks.

She entered her classroom. The door closed behind her, and

she leaned against it. Tears finally came. Tears for the Harold she had once known. Tears for Jim, who no longer cared.

 за

When Ruth arrived home, Alma was straightening the house and setting out teacups and plates of cookies. "Hazel Ellison and Grace Schumaker will be here any minute, Ruth. You're welcome to join us."

"Sorry to miss your party, Gram, but I'm off to notify people about the scrap drive—ones living too far out for the kids to reach on their bikes. I need to get it done before school starts." She headed for the door. "Have a good time."

She got in the car and checked the list of names. "Womacks are the closest," she said aloud as she pulled out onto Woodland Avenue and headed north, turning off on a dirt road that wound through the wooded countryside. A small white house, its paint flaking and peeling, came up on the left, and she turned into the driveway. In the backyard she could see the rusting remains of old bedsprings, an icebox, and a car that had died long ago. Chickens wandered about the weedy yard, and a goat stared at her over a fence as she got out of the car.

"Uh-oh!" she exclaimed as two geese gave loud honks, lowered their heads, and came at her. She raced for the porch, then jumped as a dog raised up on the steps with a howl, sniffing at her suspiciously as she climbed the stairs.

"I'm not sure this is safer," she muttered, looking around. The sagging porch was covered with an old mattress on which slept a cat and six kittens. Old newspapers were strewn about. Flies buzzed, flying in and out of a screen door that had more screen torn and hanging than attached to the wooden frame. "You'd think they could fix it," she criticized, "and clean up the mess."

She knocked loudly and soon heard footsteps scuffing across the floor. A woman's face appeared in the doorway, her long, dull brown hair stringy and unkempt, and her faded dress hanging like a sack on her very thin frame. On her feet she wore old blue slippers.

"Mrs. Womack?" Ruth inquired. *The woman looks as neglected as the rest of the place,* she thought, as she stared at the figure before her.

The woman nodded as a small girl came up from behind and grabbed her around the legs. Ruth stared at the thin, shy child. A baby could be heard coughing and fussing in the background.

"I'm Ruth Sinclair, ma'am." She went on to explain the reason for her visit. "I noticed a pile of metal scraps in your backyard. Would you be willing to contribute?"

The woman shifted uncomfortably. "Ben's not been well. Don't think he could get the stuff hauled. Truck died anyhow," she answered shortly.

Ruth watched the forlorn-looking pair before her. "I can send trucks out to pick up anything you're willing to contribute, Mrs. Womack. And the government will pay you for it, too."

She could see the woman considering the offer and the small glint of hope that lit in her eyes. "Pay us? For junk?"

"Yes, ma'am. Haven't you heard of the country's scrap drives—metal, rubber, paper, and old cloth?"

The woman sighed and shook her head. "Don't take the paper no more and don't have a radio. Electricity's off anyhow." She looked defeated. "Ben's been sick and the baby, too, but we can't afford no doctor. Sure could use some money."

Ruth took a deep breath. A wave of guilt came over her for the quick judgments she'd made as the Womacks' situation sank in. "The government will pay you well for all you can give," she explained as she thought quickly. "And since you don't have a car, maybe the men could take your husband to the doctor when they pick up the scraps. If he can get some help, he could be able to work again."

The woman picked up the little girl and stepped out on the porch. "There's lots more junk down in our gully. Old cars and tires and stuff rustin'. You can take it all." She pointed to an area beyond the pasture where Ruth could see the tip of a large pile of rusting metal. "People from all over dumped their junk in there for years. Never thought it would be any use."

"It is now, Mrs. Womack. If you sell it, you'll help your country and your family." Ruth smiled at the little girl who had buried her face in her mother's shoulder and peered at Ruth out of one eye.

"Times have been hard," Mrs. Womack explained. "Things went bad when Ben hurt his leg. And then he got sick. Only had the garden and animals to keep us fed. Don't know what we'll do when winter comes." The grim, tense look returned to her face.

"With so much scrap material to sell, I think you can start getting back on your feet." Ruth stopped to slap at a fly buzzing about her. "If you agree, I'll have the men out here this week."

The woman nodded.

Ruth smiled at the girl. "Your folks'll get paid for the scraps, and then I'll have some ladies from our church give you and your mama a ride to the grocery store."

The woman took a deep breath. "My grandma took me to church when I was a girl. Church had a piano, and we sang so nice." A longing came into her voice. "It's been so long. Ben weren't never one for church."

"If you want to go, I'll see to it," Ruth assured the mother quickly. "Someone can pick you up on Sunday. We have a piano, and the people love to sing."

Mrs. Womack smiled for the first time and looked at Ruth with tears in her eyes. "I been prayin' for help. Didn't think we mattered enough He'd bother, though." She wiped at her eyes. "Maybe He does care." She hugged the little girl tightly as tears rolled down her cheeks.

"God cares, Mrs. Womack," Ruth assured her. "He led me here. I know He did." She blinked her eyes and walked carefully down the sagging porch steps. "I have to get to the other houses around here. Expect the trucks out tomorrow or the next day. I'll arrange to have someone take you to town, too."

She waved at the two as they watched her leave.

She got in her car and sat there. "Lord, forgive me for judging before I knew anything about them. And thank You for using me to give them hope in spite of my attitude. I take so much for granted in my life." She sat a moment, then went on to finish her calls.

❧

That evening Ruth described her visit to the Womacks. "I almost cried, Gram. They'd lost hope."

Alma shook her head. "I'll get the Ladies Aid out there tomorrow. We'll bring food to get them by and some supplies to help clean up. And we can certainly spare some of the clothes we've collected so they're decently dressed." She got up and turned. "The Proctors live out that way. I'll see if they can give them a ride to church." She headed for the phone to make the arrangements.

George sat quietly in his chair. "Sounds like they got so far down they couldn't see up," he said finally. "I'll get some men out to look at Ben's truck. Could be they'll need some wood cut, too, if Ben's laid up. Lord expects us to help when we can."

"It's all set," Alma said as she came back into the room. "The ladies will be out tomorrow. I'll go see what I can put together. Trucks can't get out there for the scraps till day after tomorrow so we'll get them through till then."

Ruth nodded. "They're a good family. Just down on their luck. With a little help they'll get back on their feet. They couldn't have made it much longer, though." She stood. "The first day of school's almost here. I'd better get busy or it'll be here before I'm ready!"

❧

On Monday afternoon Alma was stirring a kettle bubbling on the stove as delicious aromas filled the kitchen. "How was your first day of school?"

Ruth sat at the table with her shoes off. "Not bad. My feet hurt and I'm tired, though. It takes getting used to every year.

I have twelve fifth-graders and eight sixth. One new student. Basically they're a good group." She nibbled on a slice of Alma's fresh bread. "How did the scrap collection go at the Womacks'?"

Alma turned with a big smile on her face. "Wonderful! They got paid well for all the scraps. Ben and the baby got the medicine they need. Grandpa found the parts for Ben's truck, and the men'll be out to help fix it. They'll stay and cut a bit of wood for them, too." She stopped to check a kettle.

"Hazel and I took Mrs. Womack and Lizbeth Ann to church for some clothes, and then we went to the grocery store. Mrs. Womack was so pleased she could buy food for the family herself. The Ladies Aid stocked their cupboards, though. They'll need plenty of good food to put on some weight. My, they're all thin!"

"And the Proctors will give them a ride to church Sunday?" Ruth inquired as she wiped crumbs from the table.

Alma nodded. "They were glad to help out. Pastor Cameron's been out to see them, too. Mr. Womack hadn't had much to do with church, but he sees all this help as an answer to his wife's prayers. His heart's open, and he's anxious to attend, too. She could never get him in a church before."

"Our actions can preach better than a dozen sermons," Ruth commented as she stood up. "I'm going to work on my blouse, Gram. Call me when I can help with dinner." She went into the dining room.

As she pinned a pattern piece on the material, she heard her grandmother's voice. "She's in the other room, Marge. Go on in."

"How's school, Teach?" Marge asked as she came in the room. "I stopped by to see if you survived the first day."

"I have no real troublemakers, so it should be a good year." She laid another pattern on the material.

"So, anything new with Jim?" Marge asked.

"Only an awkward meeting last week." Ruth stopped and recounted the teachers' meeting. "Now that he has someone else, why am I still so hung up on him? I've prayed about it and gotten after myself."

"You've never admitted how hard you fell." Marge paused and looked thoughtful. "I've seen Jim and that woman together around town. They're an odd couple. She clings to his arm, but he doesn't seem too thrilled. He's too serious. Not the old friendly, teasing Jim."

Ruth nodded. "I've noticed that, too, but I thought he was just uncomfortable because he led me on."

"They don't seem like a well-matched couple. Unlike Jack and me." Marge grinned and flashed her ring.

Ruth sat back on the floor. "Jim's Friday night Bible studies are coming up soon," she said with a sigh. "I don't look forward to an evening with him—or maybe even him and her—but after I called all the people and urged them to come, how can I back out? Don't forget you promised to come with me, Marge. I don't want to face it alone."

Marge wrinkled her nose. "I'm not that much into Bible study. Sunday morning's okay, but. . ."

Ruth gave her friend a fierce scowl. "No excuses, Marge. It'll be good for you—and for our friendship!"

seventeen

"What a perfect fall day to get the place ready for winter!" Ruth declared as she and George pulled into the Nakamuras' driveway. "Indian summer for sure." The sky was deep blue with white fluffy clouds. The air was mild with a hint of coolness and the smell of burning leaves.

She looked around. "People from church have helped keep the yard looking nice this summer."

George nodded. "And we had a good fruit harvest, too. With everyone's help we had a handsome profit to put in Suzi and Nak's bank account." He picked up the box of cleaning supplies and followed Ruth to the porch. She unlocked the door, then jumped back and screeched as something leaped at her.

George chuckled. " 'Fraid you'll get eaten by Fluffy?"

"She startled me!" Ruth exclaimed indignantly. "What in the world were you doing in there, Fluffy? How did you get in? You were at our house for dinner last night."

"She's not talking." George smiled. "Must have a way to sneak in. Check the windows while you're in there."

"There's nothing open. Someone had to let her in," Ruth insisted. "I tell you, strange things are going on here. If someone's trying to irritate us, it's working! But it makes me even more determined not to give up!"

"We won't solve it standing here, and the sheriff's not concerned," George replied. "Let's get to work."

Ruth went through the house, checking all the windows, and found nothing open. She shook her head in irritation as she pulled a sheet over the sofa to protect it from dust.

Her thoughts drifted to the Bible study and on to Jim. *Does everything in life have to be a puzzle? Now Jim's one, too. He and that woman don't match. Or am I wishing?*

George appeared in the doorway. "It's odd. Last time I checked there were five pigeons. Now there are ten!"

"I keep telling you strange things are going on here, Grandpa."

"Don't know what it's all about. Someone's trying to rattle us, I guess." He shook his white head. "I'm done back there. You ready?"

She nodded and closed up the house.

"Where do you think the Nakamuras are, Grandpa?" Ruth asked as they climbed into the car for the drive home. "I was sure they'd be back by now."

George cleared his throat and paused, glancing at her. "Gabriel Heatter's broadcast the other night said all Japanese have been relocated off the West Coast—Utah and Wyoming and places like that—so they can't spy or signal the enemy. Grandma didn't want to upset you."

"Oh, no," Ruth whispered. "I've been so busy I haven't been catching the news. How can this be happening in America?" She slumped down in her seat.

"People are afraid. They don't trust the Lord. But the Nakamuras do. We need to, too," George said as he pulled into their driveway.

≈

On Sunday morning, Tim bounded into the Sunday school classroom where Ruth was going over the attendance list. "Hey, Miss Sinclair, you teaching our class?" he asked as he looked through the pile of lessons she had set down on the table.

"Yes; Mrs. Everett got sick and can't finish the quarter," Ruth replied and picked up the lessons before Tim mixed them up.

"This isn't real school, so I don't have to watch my English here," he declared. "We learn about God stuff. I like the story about David and Goliath best. Me and Charlie wanna make slingshots and practice with stones, like David. Then we'll be ready to catch spies!"

Ruth let the comment slide as she placed a lesson at each child's place.

"Hey, Miss Sinclair, did you know Mr. Griffin's plant has trouble with spies?" Tim chattered on. "They're bringing in the army and the sheriff. Me and Charlie are on the case, too. We'll give 'em our clues!" He sat down and placed a book on the table in front of him. "Oh, yeah, we found this book by the plant. Charlie says it's yours. Here." He handed her Suzi's copy of *Ben-Hur.*

Ruth took it in surprise. "You found it outside Mr. Griffin's plant? What was it doing there?" She turned it over in her hands. The cover showed only slight damage from the damp ground.

Tim shrugged. "We just found it on the ground. We were looking for spies, and Charlie stepped on it."

"Thanks, Tim. I'm very glad to get it back. I borrowed it from a friend and felt so bad I'd lost it. Tell Charlie thanks, too." She paged through it. *Someone's been marking in it,* she noticed. *I'll have to get that erased.*

The door opened as several children walked in and clustered around Tim. Ruth put the book with her purse and turned to start the class.

❧

On Friday night, Ruth and Marge entered the church basement for Jim's Bible study. People milled about, talking in small groups as they waited for the class to begin. Ruth could see familiar faces here and there.

"I'm surprised to see so many people," Marge commented as she looked at the group.

"Times are hard. They're looking for answers," Ruth replied and glanced around the room.

"She's over there. By the kitchen," Marge whispered.

Ruth turned casually and took a good look at her competition. *Wearing slacks and a blouse cut a bit too low,* she observed. *Very pretty, but she looks out of place here.* The woman was surveying the crowd and caught Ruth staring at her. When she smiled confidently, Ruth looked away quickly.

Jim walked over to the circle of chairs set up at one end of the room. "Please take a seat and let's get started," he called out over the conversations. People turned toward the chairs and found places to sit.

"This way, Marge." Ruth hurried for seats that wouldn't be directly across from Jim. The woman sat down next to him, a Bible in her lap.

"I'm pleased to see so many here tonight. Since we have people from all over the area, let's go around the circle and give our names," Jim said after an opening prayer.

Ruth listened carefully as the woman's turn came and she said, "Carolyn Samuels."

Jim opened his Bible. "Our topic tonight is one that's affecting all our lives right now—fear."

"You said it, Jim!" Tom Adams piped up. "Everyone's scared with this war on. All those people gettin' killed overseas. . ."

"Yeah," Bill Smith interrupted, "God says He answers prayer and helps us, but people over there prayed, and look what's happenin' to 'em anyway. A guy'd be crazy not to be scared." He slumped back in his chair.

Jim smiled. "I can see this was a good topic to start with." He paged through his Bible. "First, let's see what God says about fear. Turn to John 14:27."

Pages rustled as the class hunted for John. Ruth turned quickly to the chapter, then watched as Carolyn Samuels fumbled with her Bible. She opened it to the front and looked around at the group. Noticing they opened it past the middle, she began paging through the book. *She doesn't look as if she's ever opened a Bible before,* Ruth thought with surprise.

"I'll read it," Deloris Fuller volunteered. " 'Peace I leave with you, my peace I give unto you: not as the world giveth, give I unto you. Let not your heart be troubled, neither let it be afraid.' "

Jim glanced around the circle. "What does Jesus say here about fear?"

Mary Brown raised her hand. Her white hair framed a gentle face. "Jesus says not to let our hearts be troubled or afraid," she answered softly. "Even in this war, Bill. In Matthew 28:20 He promises He'll always be with us." She smiled at him kindly.

Bill looked sheepish. "I know, but I'm still afraid my friends will be killed overseas or my family bombed here. I want God to protect us, not just be with us. I don't feel like I can count on Him to do that even if I ask Him." He ran his fingers through his hair, leaving strands sticking up here and there.

"Me, either," Tom agreed as he fingered the cuff of his blue-plaid flannel shirt. "If I can't trust Him to keep awful things from happening, how can I help being afraid?"

Murmurs buzzed around the circle. Ruth glanced toward Jim to see him listening intently to the comments.

"I think the answer lies in what we're trusting Him for," Jean Preston spoke up. "Do we trust Him only to do what we want, or do we trust Him just because He's God?"

"That first part's me," Tom confessed. "Trust is hard for me because I don't really believe He'll always do what I want."

"Whew!" Bill shook his head. "I'm afraid if I trust Him to do what He wants, He'll make me do something I won't like—sort of like having to eat liver and onions." He shuddered. "It's supposed to be good for me, but, ugh!"

The class chuckled. Ruth glanced at Carolyn to see her stifling a yawn, and she remembered the woman Jim said he stopped dating in California because she wasn't a Christian. *His beliefs haven't changed,* she thought. *I don't understand why he's with someone who seems so uninterested in God.*

Jim leaned forward with his arms on his knees. "Remember, since the Fall, there's sin and evil in this world. Believers live in the world and feel the effects of that evil. We'd like God to put a wall around us as soon as we believe, so nothing bad will touch us, but it isn't that way."

"The lives of the disciples certainly illustrate that," Jean declared firmly as she smoothed her skirt. "They suffered for the gospel."

"They did," Jim agreed. "Now turn to John 16:33." Pages rustled as he continued. "Jesus tells the disciples that in Him they can have peace, whatever happens. He says in this world we will have tribulations or troubles, but we're to be of good cheer because He has overcome the world."

"So, Jesus is saying the world will always be a mess." Tom sounded discouraged.

An elderly man sitting next to Carolyn cleared his throat. "Jesus gives us His peace," he began quietly, "not the way the world tries to by winnin' wars and treaties and gettin' lots of money and such." He looked around. "It's by trustin' Him with our lives because He's God that we can have peace in our hearts no matter what happens." He kept fingering one side of his mustache.

The room grew quiet as he continued. "I've lived a long time, and I've seen people try a lotta things to get peace." He shook his white head. "Doesn't work. People just waste their years trying to find peace on the outside. Trusting Jesus with our hearts. That's where peace is." He sat back. "Didn't mean to say so much."

The quiet continued as his words sank in.

Bill squirmed in his chair. "Guess I got it all backwards. I wanted life to be peaceful all around me, and then I'd get peace inside. Sounds like God works from the inside out." He looked around for confirmation.

Ruth nodded. "You're right, Bill. If we don't trust Him and His will, we'll never have peace in our hearts. But it isn't trust when I ask God to do His will and then tell Him how He's to do it. It's hard to give up insisting that things be done my way, especially in a war, but to me that's what trusting God means. But it's not an easy lesson to learn," she admitted.

Jim smiled at her warmly and held her gaze. "We've come to that critical point where we all have to struggle every day of our lives: Trust God to do as He sees best, even if things aren't going the way we want at the moment. It's not easy to accept that, especially in bad times like this, but it's something we have to grow in if we want peace inside instead of fear. We learn it best in the hard times. God makes good use of them. In the hard times ahead in this war, there will be many opportunities to grow in trust and leave our fears behind. Don't let them slip by." He glanced at his watch. "On that we'll stop for tonight. Let's close with prayer."

After the amen, Ruth pulled on Marge's arm and whispered, "Let's go before Jim comes by."

As they hurried from the room, Marge looked puzzled. "Did you see that woman with Jim? She didn't know where The Book of John was. And when we were reading, she looked as if she couldn't believe intelligent people would actually swallow all this. I don't get it—Jim and her, I mean."

"I thought it was just me," Ruth agreed.

As they walked to the coatrack, Marge continued. "I thought Bible studies were boring talks about living way back when people were living in tents and wearing robes and riding camels. This applies to us now. It has to do with our lives. I'm surprised." She handed Ruth her coat.

"That's the beauty of the Bible," Ruth replied. "No matter when you live, it speaks to you. God wrote it that way."

"I guess I've never really read it. We learned stories in Sunday school, but my folks weren't into reading it, so I thought it was for kids and sermons on Sunday. Not for getting along in the world." Marge paused to rebutton her coat correctly.

"When we think we can handle life, we put God on a shelf, Marge. When it gets rough, we're willing to take a look at what He has to say to us." She remembered her conversation with Jim on that topic. "I'm a good example of that."

"You? How?" Marge asked, puzzled. They stood in the entry talking as voices floated up from conversations downstairs.

"I worry about my life and where it's going. About Harold, my feelings for Jim, the war. I'm afraid my faith and trust have been very shallow."

"Then where does that leave me?" Marge looked concerned.

"I still think He should straighten out the mess this world's in—and Jim and that woman."

"He's just waiting till we realize we can't handle things so we'll listen to Him. I struggle here. Especially since I can't seem to get Jim out of my heart," she declared with a tone of discouragement.

As they stepped from the church, George drove out of the parking lot and pulled up to the door. "Just like taxi service," Marge quipped and got in the car.

"How was Bible study?" Alma inquired as they pulled out onto the road.

"Excellent." Ruth related the evening's discussion as they drove to the Evans's and dropped Marge off.

"We had a lovely time at the Hoeffers'," Alma commented. "She's a wonderful cook and even makes war recipes taste delicious."

"I agree there," George concurred and pulled into their driveway. "Um, that pie! But, Alma, my dear, your crust is flakier." He winked at Ruth as he climbed the steps and opened the door. "I didn't want to sleep in the barn tonight," he whispered.

"I heard that, George Peterson." Alma followed him into the house.

George chuckled and whistled down the hall to their room.

"That man!" Alma smiled at Ruth. "I pray you'll be as blessed someday! Good night and sleep well, dear."

eighteen

The steady tick of the clock echoed in the otherwise silent kitchen. Ruth placed her Bible and purse on the table, sat down, and put her head in her hands. "Lord, so many strange things are happening." Tears ran down her cheeks. "I admit it, Lord. I've fallen in love with Jim Griffin, and now it's too late. This lesson in trust is a hard one. Help me."

She sat a moment, wiped her eyes, and got up. *A good sleep will help,* she thought as she climbed the stairs to her room. She pushed the door open and turned on the light. "Oh, what's happened?" she gasped. Books lay scattered all over the floor. Dresser drawers were ransacked and clothes strewn about the room.

She ran to the top of the stairs. "Grandma, Grandpa, come up here! Something's happened!" she hollered.

Lights flicked on below as her grandparents hurried from their room. "What's the matter, Ruth?" George called as he rushed up the stairs.

"Are you sick?" Alma followed behind.

"Someone's been in my room and torn it up." Her face was white and her hands shook. She pointed through the doorway. "Look! I walked in and found it like this."

George and Alma stood frozen in astonishment at the mess in Ruth's room. "This is no prank. I'm getting the sheriff's men out here," George said grimly. "Don't touch anything." He hurried downstairs.

Ruth and Alma stood in the hallway, staring in disbelief at the mess.

George came up behind them. "His men'll be right here." He shook his head at the disaster.

"I don't understand," Ruth spoke dazedly. "I don't have

anything worth stealing. I haven't done anything to anyone. Why would someone do this?"

At a sharp rap on the front door, George hurried down the stairs.

"I'll go put the teakettle on. A cup of hot tea will do you good. Will you be okay, dear?" Alma asked. Ruth nodded.

"She turned on the light and found the room as it is," George was saying as he escorted two officers up the stairs. "This is my granddaughter, Ruth Sinclair." They nodded a greeting. "We were out for the evening. It happened while we were gone. And we locked the doors before we left."

The two officers stepped into the room and looked around. One gave a low whistle. "Some mess!"

George put his arm around Ruth. "Go down to the kitchen for something warm to drink while the officers do their job." Alma met them at the top of the stairs. "You go with her," George said. "I'm staying up here. I want to be nearby in case they have any questions."

Alma followed Ruth into the kitchen and bustled about preparing the tea. They could hear the men talking and moving around upstairs.

"This house has always seemed so safe from the dangers of the rest of the world," Ruth said as she sat down. "Someone's taking that away."

Alma poured two cups of tea. "We have to learn it over and over, but there's only one safe place, one secure refuge, and that's the Lord."

Ruth nodded. "I'm getting that lesson, but no more homework on it, please." She smiled weakly.

One of the officers appeared in the doorway. "May I use your phone, ma'am?"

"It's in the hall," Alma directed.

Ruth sipped her tea. "First it was the bookcase at school, then the one at Suzi's and all the strange things happening there. Someone stole my purse and *Ben-Hur,* and now this. I have nothing valuable to steal, nothing secret. It has to be harassment, Gram, because I won't desert my Japanese friends." She searched for some logical answer.

"Miss, you can go up and straighten your things. We need to check out the downstairs and talk to your grandparents." The officers came into the kitchen with George.

"Go ahead, Ruth. You'll feel better with your things straightened up," Alma urged.

Upstairs, she looked at the jumble of clothes and books. As she began sorting out the clothes and putting them back in the drawers and closet, she could hear a rap at the living room door and someone hurrying to open it. The voices moved to the steps, then footsteps came up the stairs and stopped at her doorway.

A familiar voice uttered a soft "Oh, no," and she looked up to see Jim standing there. Her mind stopped in confusion. "What are you doing here?" she blurted.

"The officers called me, and I came right over." He jingled the coins in his pocket, his face showing concern and anger as he surveyed the mess.

She looked puzzled. "But why would they call you for this? The sheriff's men are here."

"We run everything unusual through civilian defense these days," he replied evasively. "Are you okay?"

She nodded and joined him in the hall. "I don't understand, Jim. Why are all these strange things happening?" She began crying.

Jim reached out and pulled her to him. "It's okay. Have a good cry." He held her close and stroked her hair. The fears and dangers melted away as she nestled in his arms. She closed her eyes.

"I have to talk to the officers. You finish straightening up here and then we'll talk." He held her away from him. "Will you be okay?" He raised her chin with his fingers and looked in her eyes. She nodded numbly and could only stare at the concern and caring in his eyes. Time seemed to freeze.

"Jim, could we see you down here?" an officer called up

the stairs, breaking the spell.

"Be right there," he returned. To Ruth he said, "Gotta go. Check carefully to see if anything's missing. We need to know."

Ruth continued putting her possessions back where they belonged. "Nothing's damaged. So far nothing seems to be missing," she muttered. She placed the last book back on the shelf and walked to the doorway. "As far as I can tell, it looks the way it did when I left for church. What was I doing before I got ready? I wrote some letters—they're on the table downstairs—and then I read *Ben*. . . Where's Suzi's book?"

She went to the bookshelves and searched through the titles, then checked under the bed and found nothing. "That seems to be all that's missing." She looked around. "Why all the fuss about that book? If they wanted the book, why did they tear up the rest of the room when the book was on the bed in plain view?"

"Ruth, could you come down here? The officers need to speak with you before they leave," Alma called up the stairs.

Downstairs, she recounted what she knew of the events.

"There's evidence the door has been jimmied," one of the officers explained. "Keep a look out for any strangers. We'll call if we have more questions." The officers stood. "Good night, folks. We're sorry this happened."

"Appreciate you checking on this," George replied. "We'll keep things locked up and our eyes open."

Alma got up from the table. "We're heading for bed. If you have any more problems, Ruth, call us."

"I love you both. Thanks." She hugged her grandparents and put the teakettle back on the stove.

Jim searched her face with concern. "I want to know everything strange that's been going on. I know you've told it all before, but maybe something new will come out. It's important."

She poured the hot tea and sat down. "You know most of it, Jim." She recounted the events that had occurred over the past months.

"Nothing else?"

She sipped her tea. "The varying number of pigeons at the Nakamuras'. Oh, and Fluffy getting locked in their house."

"Go on."

"Jim, the strangest thing is *Ben-Hur*. I borrowed it from Suzi's. It's the only thing missing upstairs. But it was on the bed in plain sight. If someone wanted it, why was my room torn apart?" She cupped her hands around the mug and thought a moment. "Oh, I forgot to tell you. Charlie and Tim have been hunting for spies and saw the lights outside your plant. When they checked on them, they found *Ben-Hur* lying on the ground beside the building. Tim brought it back to me."

Jim's head jerked up. "You should have told me."

Ruth shrugged. "It didn't seem important. What's going on, Jim?"

He took her hand. "I can't tell you much. You've heard rumors our plant has been converted to war production?"

She nodded.

"It's true. And we've had some shipments broken into. We want to find out who's doing it, not just scare them off so they move on to cause trouble someplace else. What connection the book has to all this I don't know. We'll try to find out."

"Don't get in any danger, Jim." Her hand tightened on his.

"I can take care of myself, but I'm worried about you. If you get the book back again, let me know right away. I want to see that book." He sat quietly looking at her hands. Then he spoke carefully. "Because I'm civilian defense coordinator for Fir Glen and because of what our plant is doing, I've gotten involved with—uh—certain parts of the government and military."

He looked down at the table. "Ruth, there's so much I'm not allowed to say. Please trust me and don't take things as they seem. I know this doesn't make sense, but it's all I can say for now." He slammed his fist into the other palm. "I feel so helpless and frustrated. I. . ." His voice drifted off. He lowered his head and shook it slowly from side to side.

"I'm sorry you have problems of this kind at the plant," she said softly. She stared across the room. "You've been a good friend, Jim. I appreciate it."

A low groan came from his lips. "Ruth, friend is a word I'm coming to dislike." He stood abruptly. "Be careful. Keep your eyes open and let me know anything unusual." He grabbed her hand and pulled her to her feet. "Get some sleep."

He looked down at her tenderly, then leaned over and kissed her cheek quickly. "I've got to go. I need to go by the plant yet tonight. I'll be praying for you." And he was gone.

"Whew!" Ruth plopped down in the chair. "That man makes my head spin and my heart pound right out of my chest, even if it's hopeless."

She stood and cleared the table. "After everything that's happened, all I can say is I'm more confused than ever."

nineteen

The October air was clear and balmy for the season with just a tinge of invigorating crispness. White fluffy clouds floated in the blue sky, and in the distance Mt. Hood stood tall and majestic with a thin mantle of new snow. Fall was putting on her annual show, painting the vine maples, dogwoods, and birches with brilliant reds, purples, oranges, and yellows.

"I do love fall!" Ruth declared as she helped her grandparents harvest the last of the vegetables from the garden.

"You said the same thing about spring," Alma chuckled. She pulled the remaining carrots in the row and shook the dirt off the roots.

"If we had just those two seasons, it would be fine with me," Ruth replied. "Spring's exciting and fall's cozy and lovely. Until it's time to pick walnuts and filberts, that is. They stain and tear the fingers so badly."

"The church'll be out to harvest Nak and Suzi's nuts soon. Then we're done over there for this year," Alma reminded her. "Your brown fingers will be right in style."

"Weather report said cloudy with showers today, so enjoy this while you can," George commented as he loaded the last pumpkin into the wheelbarrow. "We'll get these in just in time. Rain's coming."

Ruth laughed as she put a crisp head of fall cabbage in her bucket. "You could predict that every morning in Oregon and be right 90 percent of the time, Grandpa."

"Now, Ruth, you know we wouldn't have this beautiful green state without all the rain," Alma chided. "Here, help me get these turnips and carrots to the house."

Ruth carried a bucket of vegetables to the faucet at the side of the house and washed off the dirt. As she walked to the porch, the wind whipped around the corner. "Grandpa's right. Something's brewing," she murmured as leaves scudded across the yard. Fluffy rubbed against her legs and purred loudly. "Head for the barn, Fluffy, or you'll get that orange fur wet."

Inside, Ruth helped her grandmother with the produce. "Grandpa will get the vegetables to the root cellar if you'll take the trimmings to the compost pile, Ruth. I'll sit a minute, and then I think I'll do some baking." Alma sat down at the table. "But first I have to see how much sugar I can use."

Ruth dumped the scraps in the compost pile behind the house and looked around her. *Such a beautiful place! Like a little bit of heaven—or at least Eden.* The tall green fir trees swayed amid the brilliant colors of fall. She looked up to see the sky overcast and the clouds darkening. *It'll be a cozy day inside. I can get some sewing done this afternoon,* she thought.

"Better head for the house before you get wet." George came up behind her, looking concerned. "My turkeys are acting strange. Piled in a big huddle. They spook easy. Storm's coming." He hurried off.

Big drops of rain began to fall as Ruth ran to the house. "Grandpa was right. It's raining," she said as Alma put a pan of cookies in the oven. "Can I help you, Gram?"

"No, dear, go ahead with your own work." She turned to knead her bread, and soon the aroma of fresh bread and cookies filled the house.

Ruth finished cutting out a winter dress and began to sew. The wind moaned around the eaves and rain pelted the windows. She looked up as the lights blinked. Wind was blowing hard, rattling the windows and whipping the trees. She heard her grandfather come in the back door, and she joined her grandparents in the kitchen.

"I got the animals in and tied down what I could. This storm could get bad. The rain's coming down hard, and that wind's strong. Better get the lamps and candles ready."

The phone rang shrilly in the hall. Alma answered it. "For

you, George. It's Wallace Coulter. He sounds anxious."

George hung up the phone after the conversation. "Wind's trying to take Coulter's chicken house roofs. He needs help. I'm loading up and heading over. Call all the men you can and get them over there right away." George pulled on his boots and donned his rain gear.

"If this lasts awhile, send the men over here for sandwiches and something hot to drink. I baked today," Alma directed.

George nodded as he hurried out the door.

"You call neighbors, Ruth, and I'll get the food ready. The men will be cold and hungry."

Ruth hurried to the phone and soon had a crew of men lined up. She went to the living room window and looked out at the storm. A dark afternoon would soon turn into a black night, and the storm raged on. The lights flickered again and then went out, leaving the house in an eerie dusk. Ruth joined her grandmother in the kitchen.

Alma was laying out cookies and sandwiches on the table. "I'm thankful I kept my old wood cookstove alongside the electric one. It warms the kitchen and is a blessing at times like this." The room was comfortable and cozy in the lamplight.

The stomping of boots sounded on the back porch, followed by a tap on the door. "Come on in," Alma called out. Three men took off their dripping rain gear and entered the kitchen. Ruth looked up in surprise as Ben Womack stepped through the door.

"Sure feels good in here," Joe Duncan said as he rubbed his hands together over the cookstove. "Nasty out."

"Sit and have some food. I'll pour hot coffee." Alma bustled over to the stove. "How's it going over there?"

"We're stacking sandbags on the roofs to hold 'em down, but the buildings are long. Takes a bunch of 'em," Arlan replied. "A lot of men turned out, but it's still a job."

"George is sending two or three of us over at a time to get a break and warm up. Sure appreciate the food, Alma. We missed supper." Joe tackled another sandwich. The three warmed their hands around the hot coffee cups.

"Cold out there," Ben spoke up, "but sure feels good to do for someone else after people was so good to us." His face looked red and chapped but healthy and filled out.

"Well, we'd best get back and let the next bunch come over. Thanks, Alma," Arlan said as he stood and walked to his rain clothes.

Shifts of men came in and out of the warm kitchen throughout the evening. "Am I thankful I baked today! The Lord sent company but a day early," Alma commented as she refilled the sandwich plate.

"Anything left for us?" The door opened and George came in followed by Jim.

"What were you doing? Playing the hero out there, George Peterson? You'll catch your death of cold. Sit down. I'll get some dry socks while you eat. Ruth, pour the men some coffee." Alma picked up a candle and hurried from the room.

"A dry shirt sounds good, too," George added. "Be right back."

Jim gave a shiver and sat down at the table. "That stove sure feels good. It's raw out there." He reached for a sandwich.

Ruth filled his cup with steaming hot coffee. "How bad is it?" She paused by the table.

"We're saving the roofs, but there'll be damage to repair. At least the chicken houses weren't blown away and the chickens with them." He helped himself to another sandwich. "Most of the men around are helping. Takes a lot of sandbags for all those long chicken houses."

Ruth looked at his wet, tousled hair, his streaked face, and damp shirt. She turned quickly for more coffee. *All I want to do is hold him close and take care of him,* she thought. *But that's not my place.*

She poured the coffee, and he looked up at her. "Thanks," he said softly. "I'll feel warmer out there remembering you like this."

She turned back to the stove. *Sure you will, Jim. Good line. I only wish it were true. But I won't fall for it again,* she thought.

With a quick rap on the door a man burst into the room, dripping water all over the floor. "Mr. Griffin, someone's broken into the plant!" he gasped, struggling to catch his breath. "It's so dark and wet I couldn't see everywhere. Jerry didn't stay for guard duty. Had to save his barn. I couldn't cover his post and mine, too. Coulter said you were over here. Phone lines are down."

Jim was on his feet and grabbing his coat. "Tell your grandpa I had an emergency." He rushed from the room.

"That feels better," George was saying as he and Alma came back into the room a few minutes later. He stopped. "Where's Jim?"

"The plant was broken into, and the guard came to get him. That's all I know."

George sat down and sipped his hot coffee. "Guess whoever it was took advantage of the weather—the lights out and all the men working on the chicken houses." He finished his sandwich and reached for his coat. "Sounds like the wind is slowing down. We may be done soon."

"Let's have a cup ourselves, Ruth. We need to sit a bit." Alma poured two cups of hot coffee and sat down with a sigh.

"I hope Jim's not in any danger." Ruth stared into the cup she was holding.

Alma looked at her sharply. "You still care, don't you, dear?" She reached for a sandwich. "I can't figure out why he's with that woman. She's not his type." They ate in silence.

"George was right. The wind is down and the rain's let up. I think the worst is over." Alma sighed and took a sip of her coffee. "Sure warmed my heart when I saw Ben come through that door. What the Lord has done in his life! He has a job at the shipyards now. And Hazel says he has a fine voice and is joining the choir."

"Thank the Lord!" Ruth declared.

"Every morning we need to ask Him to help us see the opportunities He puts in front of us," Alma said firmly. "When

I think what would have happened to that family if you hadn't stopped by. . ." Alma shook her head.

As they cleaned up, the kitchen door opened, and George stepped into the room. "We saved 'em. I'm going to change out of these wet clothes and then come back for some hot coffee." He picked up a candle and left the room.

Alma was pouring three cups of hot coffee as George came back in dry clothes and sat down to recount the evening's work. "We thought we'd lose one roof," he related. "There'd have been chickens and feathers blown from here to the Cascade Mountains, but the sandbags held it down." He shook his head. "Wind 'bout blew us off the roof, and rain came in our faces so hard we couldn't see."

There was a light tap at the door, and Jim stepped into the warm kitchen.

"Everything all right?" George asked as he looked up between sips.

Jim pulled up a chair. "Someone broke into the office and went through the files. There were papers all over the floor. We don't know what they found, but we'll have to alter our shipping schedules and put on more guards." He ran his fingers through his hair. "I came over tonight because of this." He placed *Ben-Hur* on the table.

"Where did you get it?" Ruth was astounded.

"It was found on the floor of the office. Apparently it was dropped and the papers scattered over it." He looked over at Ruth. "I need to keep it for a while. It's time we found out why there's been so much fuss over this book—and why it was at our plant."

Ruth nodded. "It's Suzi's, but you can keep it for now."

"Did you have much damage?" George inquired. He wrapped his hands around the hot cup.

"No damage. Just a mess of papers. There are people interested in what we produce and where we ship it. With a war on, the enemy wants to know the country's military and industrial output." Jim paused and looked at a napkin he folded as he talked. "I'm not at liberty to explain much. War restrictions."

The other three nodded.

"The way things are today," George commented.

"I was disturbed to find the book dropped by whoever broke into the plant." Jim turned the book over in his hands. "It was probably the same person who ransacked your bedroom, Ruth, and your classroom and Suzi's house. We don't know the connection yet, but if I keep the book, they shouldn't bother you about it. They know where they lost it."

"Why would someone want that book?" Alma asked. "It's a religious story."

"I don't know yet." He leaned back in his chair.

Ruth commented, "The only other person connected with the book was that dark-haired man at the café. He stared at me that day while I read it. And then he grabbed it and ran off with it. But if he wanted it so badly, why did he throw it down? Remember, Jim, you found it."

Jim nodded. "You never discovered who he was?"

Ruth shook her head. "I haven't seen him since. He's probably not around here anymore."

"It's late." Jim stood up. "You people need some sleep, and I have to get back to the plant. There's a lot to do so this can't happen again." He picked up his hat. "The war's complicating life everywhere."

"But the Lord's with us," George said softly. "The world may be going crazy, but there can still be peace inside for believers."

The room was quiet as his words sank in.

"We need to pray and trust the Lord," Jim agreed as he put on his hat and opened the door. "Good night, all."

❧

On Friday night, Ruth rushed around dusting the living room furniture and plumping the pillows. "Thanks for letting us hold the Bible study here tonight," she said as she straightened the doilies on the end tables.

"Church basement'll be a mess for a while yet," George

commented. "That wind took the shingles right off the roof, and then the rain poured in. Takes time to dry out."

Alma brought in another chair. "I worry there won't be enough seats for everyone, dear," she fussed.

"We'll have enough. Some of the people canceled. They had to clean up their own storm damage," Ruth explained.

A rap on the door sent Alma scurrying to admit Jim and three other class members. "Come in and have a seat," she urged as she took their coats. They sat down and chatted about the storm as a few more drifted in.

Ruth's heart gave a skip when Jim greeted her, and she hurried to the kitchen. Marge entered the room as she was piling Alma's corn-syrup cookies on a platter.

"There you are, hiding out in here," Marge teased. She picked up a plate of cookies and carried it to the dining room behind her friend. "He's here by himself again," she whispered. "Carolyn's missed the last two Bible studies. I told you she looked bored."

"Shh," Ruth whispered back. "Someone'll hear." She put down the plates of cookies.

"Okay, let's get started," Jim called out. "Our group will be smaller tonight, so we won't wait any longer." The class settled down and attention turned to Jim as Ruth took a seat next to Marge.

"This week we're going to talk about choices," Jim announced. "Let's start by taking a look at the first choice mankind faced and the decision that was made. Of course I'm referring to Adam and Eve. God gave them a choice. What was that choice, and what did they do?"

Art Fuller piped up. "They chose a red delicious apple! I saw it on the front of my Sunday school lesson when I was a kid," he joked. "Made me scared to eat apples for years!"

The class laughed.

"Reminds me of the apple the wicked queen gave Snow White in my daughter's storybook," he continued. "It was poison!"

Jim chuckled along with the group. "Actually you're not far off, Art. Their choice was a poison we call sin, and it did cause death. But turn to Genesis and let's go back. . ."

Ruth watched the faces in the group as they eagerly responded to Jim's discussion. *Choices, great!* she thought. *A fine topic for me! Seems like I've been making wrong choices this whole year. If only I'd told Harold. . .* She glanced at Jim as he listened intently to Jean Preston's comment. *He made a choice, too—and it wasn't me! I hope Carolyn realizes how fortunate she is to have a man like Jim. But why can't he get her to Bible study anymore?* she wondered.

She could feel Jim looking at her. "And what do you think, Ruth?"

Her face grew warm as she tried to remember what they were talking about. "Would you repeat that, Jim?"

"You looked so deep in thought I was sure you had some words of wisdom." He smiled at her and reviewed the last comment. "Mary said our choices are important because what we choose can affect the spiritual lives of others. Can you elaborate on that?"

Ruth swallowed hard. "The world's full of darkness today," she began uncertainly, hoping she was on the topic. "In our choices we can either contribute to the darkness or be a light shining for Christ. We must choose to stay close to the Lord so He can shine through our lives to others."

"Sounds like a tall order to me," Art admitted. "Don't think I'd be a very big light, dark as the world is now."

Ruth nodded. "Me neither, but that's where the whole church comes in. One candle doesn't give a lot of light, but a whole bunch of candles can make a great light. That's what the church is to be—a lot of little reflectors of Jesus making a light big enough to dispel the darkness. Staying close enough to Him that we reflect Him—that's a very important choice."

"Yeah," Tom Adams added. "Guess if more people had followed God, we wouldn't be in this awful war. Sure makes me think about how careful we need to be!"

"You've wrapped it up well. Remember, when we choose to read the Word and pray or not, when we make a choice to obey or disobey God, it makes a difference. Ask God to help in what you choose." He closed his Bible and smiled at Ruth. "Let's close with prayer."

As the group rose from their seats, Alma called out, "Help yourselves to cookies in the dining room."

Ruth waited as the line formed. A sudden rap at the door jolted her, and she hurried to open it. There stood Carolyn Samuels smiling at her.

"I'm sorry to interrupt, but I need to speak to Jim," Carolyn was saying as Ruth looked at the lovely woman before her. Her hair and clothes were the latest style, and everything about her was modern and immaculate. Unconsciously Ruth patted her simple hairdo and looked down at her worn shoes.

"Come in. I'll get him for you." She closed the door behind Carolyn and worked her way through the group to Jim, a sinking feeling settling over her. *I hadn't seen Carolyn for a while,* she thought. *I guess I hoped. . .*

"Jim," she said as she approached him, "there's someone at the door to see you." She watched him glance that direction and a knowing look come over his face. He nodded and hurried to the entryway, where Carolyn waited. They talked a moment; then Jim headed for the pile of coats and rummaged through for his. He quickly thanked Alma for her hospitality and followed Carolyn out the door.

Ruth gave a shiver. The room suddenly seemed empty.

"What was that all about?" Marge came up behind her.

Ruth shrugged. "I guess she came to pick him up."

"Don't look so down, Ruth. I'm still working on your love life, but it's hard these days with all the men going off to war." Marge stepped to the doorway and hesitated. Her face grew serious. "Pray for Jack and me, Ruth. I'm so scared he'll be shipped overseas when he gets his new orders." She blinked her eyes, then quickly slipped out the door.

twenty

Alma plopped into a kitchen chair on a fall Saturday afternoon. "My, it's good to sit down!" She rubbed her sore fingers stained brown from the walnut harvest at the Nakamuras'.

"We picked a lot of nuts. Glad so many people from the church showed up to help," George commented as he washed up.

Ruth busied herself putting away food left from the noon potluck that had fed the pickers. She looked around. "Gram, where's the roast? I don't see it here."

"Last I saw, it was on Suzi's stove in the roaster. Hazel was cutting it into sandwich meat. There was plenty left, though." She looked at George. "Anything more in the truck?"

"Nope," he replied. "Brought it all in."

"Fine day to be forgetful," Alma sighed. "With all the work we did I thought it would make a quick and easy supper."

"I'll go get it, Grandma. The walk will be a good way to unwind." Ruth slipped into her coat. "You two rest while I'm gone. You deserve it. In fact, I hear those overstuffed chairs in the living room calling you."

Ruth ambled down the path, humming as she crossed the field. The late afternoon sun cast long shadows across the ground in its descent behind the fir trees bordering the field. *A lot of sore backs today, but it feels good to know we didn't let any of Nak's crops go to waste this year,* she thought as she enjoyed the glow of fading sunlight.

As she approached the farmhouse steps, Fluffy let out a meow and bounded to meet her. "Just because you got lunch here today doesn't mean there'll be supper here, too. You have to come home with me for that," she said to the cat as she mounted the stairs.

The screen door gave a loud squeak as she pulled it open. The door stood ajar. "I should have checked it before I left," she scolded herself. "Good thing I came back." She pushed the door open and walked toward the stove, pausing at the table.

"Who did this?" she demanded. On the table lay Suzi's bookmarks, a strip of paper with a listing of Bible verses, and an open book. "I told the kids not to play with these this morning, but someone didn't listen. Suzi's bookmarks are too special to be used as toys." She crumpled up the strip of paper and stuffed it in her pocket. "And look. They marked all over Suzi's book." She picked it up along with the bookmarks. "I'll take it home and get these marks erased."

"Well, well, well, if it ain't the teacher," a deep voice spoke behind her.

A jolt of fear ran through her as she turned to see a dark-haired man with a scraggly beard coming into the room. "I told ya to git back home once, but ya didn't listen." He glared at her. "Can't you learn nothin'?"

Ruth opened her mouth, but no sound came out.

The man strode to the table. "Leave our stuff alone." He grabbed the book and bookmarks from her. "The paper, too," he demanded as he held out his hand. "Git in here, Leland," he barked toward the hall. "We got work to do."

Leland Hinson slinked into the room and slid into a chair at one side of the table.

"Sit!" the man ordered Ruth. "We don't have no time to bother with you now. Boss'll be here soon." He pulled a tiny piece of paper from his pocket and reached out to turn the pages in the Bible. Then he took one of Suzi's bookmarks from the pile and started to write on it.

"No, you can't do that! Those aren't yours." Ruth was shocked to hear the sound of her own voice.

The man glared at her. "You gonna stop me?" he snarled. "Shut up! We got coding to do. Leland, git out and see if the last message is in. We need it to git this done."

Leland soon returned with a tiny capsule. "Last bird was

in," he said as he handed it to his cousin.

A wave of fear hit Ruth. "You're the ones who took the pigeons," she gasped. "You're spies!"

"Smart lady. Leland, the teacher can add two and two," the man said sarcastically.

Leland glanced at the clock on the wall. "Boss'll be here soon, Bert." He shifted nervously in his seat. "What'll we do with her? Boss won't be happy." He licked his lips, and his eyes flicked from Bert to Ruth. "Boss gits mean, real mean, if things ain't right."

Lord, Ruth prayed desperately, *help me. Show me what to do. Bring someone to help me. Please!*

Bert picked up the book and began underlining words here and there.

She caught her breath. "You're the one who marked in *Ben-Hur* and kept stealing it!"

Leland snickered. "Boss was sure mad 'bout that Ben book. Had the code list on the bookmark in it, too. Told Bert to git 'em both back or else. But Bert's dumb. Threw the book away the first time just cause the bookmark warn't in it. Boss was in a fit!"

"Shut up, Leland." He glared at his cousin. "You're the one lost the book twice."

"Bert's got a nasty temper. Tears things up. Boss was mad he left a mess looking for it. Made people suspicious."

Ruth squeezed her shaking hands together.

"Boss'll pay us soon," Leland rambled. "Can git my farm back. Chase them foreigners out, and there'll be room for us real Americans." He rambled on as Ruth sat terrified.

Keep him talking, she thought. *Stall for time. Someone will come looking for me if I'm gone too long.*

"Spies must get a lot of money," she managed to squeak out.

Leland nodded and grinned. "Easy work, too. Just sneak around and find out what's goin' on. Bert met Boss in Californy. Boss said we could make a lot of money if we helped. Government ain't done me no good, and I sure could use the money." He glanced at the clock again.

Greedy and scared. I wonder if he knows how much trouble he's in. An idea formed in her mind. "You must be very brave to be a spy," she ventured.

"Nah, just sneak around. Easy."

"But it's so dangerous. If you get caught you could be executed, you know." She forced a look of concern.

Leland frowned and his eyes got bigger. "Bert said spies don't git no more 'n a few days in jail. No big deal."

"The government caught eight German spies on the East Coast this summer. They executed six of them on August 8 and two went to prison." Ruth watched his face carefully.

"Tell her, Bert. Spies just get a few days in jail." She could hear the fear creeping into his voice.

"Don't pay her no attention," Bert growled. "We ain't gittin' caught. Leave me alone. Got to git this coding done."

Panic crossed Leland's face. "I ain't gittin' killed, Bert, and I don't wanna go to prison. All I want's my farm back," he whined and swallowed hard.

From the look on his face, Ruth could tell he saw the same movement she did. Their eyes stared at the window.

"I saw something out there, Bert. Like a face," Leland whispered.

Bert snorted. "Dumb cousin. You believe in ghosts?"

As he glanced at Leland, a face flashed by the window, vague in the deepening dusk. Bert shoved his chair back and dashed out the door, searching around the house, then storming back in. "Nothin' there. Just gittin' spooked. Now leave me alone." He looked at the clock. "Got to hurry this. Boss'll be here." He settled back to work on the coding.

Leland jerked his head toward his cousin. "Bert can do a lotta things. He can break in anywhere. Best counterfeiter in these here parts, too. He. . ."

All three heads swung around as footsteps sounded on the porch. Then there was silence. Bert rose and moved stealthily to the door. He stepped outside and searched around.

"Didn't see no one. Musta been the wind. Gittin' spooked." He frowned as he returned to the table.

Leland's face had turned pale. "Can't be the boss. Boss won't come while we're here. Have to signal when we leave. Maybe someone's onto us." He shoved his chair back. "Don't want no money, Bert. You can have it all. Don't want to git killed. I'm outta here!" He rushed to the door and out into the night before Bert could react.

Ruth watched tensely as Bert glanced at the clock and swore. "Dumb cousin. No help anyway." He looked up again at the window and grabbed the papers to finish his coding. As he put the items away, the bookmark he had worked on slid to the floor and under the table. He placed the book and the rest of the bookmarks back on the shelf.

"I ain't gonna worry about you. Leave that to the boss." He took out a piece of rope and pulled her hands behind the chair. He tied the knots tightly, then tied each ankle to a chair leg. "You're not runnin' off and bringing the sheriff to ruin my deal." He gave the rope a yank as Ruth flinched in pain.

"Teachers talk too much. This'll keep you quiet." He pulled a rag out of his pocket and tied it around her mouth. "Always wanted to do that when I was in school." He smiled grimly and glanced around the room. "That's what ya git for not listenin', Teach." He picked up his flashlight. "Time to signal the boss." He slipped out the door and was gone.

Ruth was left in silent darkness as she fought a wave of panic. *Why hasn't anyone wondered where I am? Why hasn't Grandpa come to check on me? I've been gone far too long.* She tried to move her arms, but the ropes were tied tight. *Lord, please send someone before the boss gets here. It'll be too late then. I'm so scared, Lord.*

Her heart pounded as another wave of panic rushed through her. *They know I can identify them. Lord, give me strength no matter what happens.*

A noise on the porch sent a jolt of fear through her. The boss. . .

The door opened quietly. In the dusk she couldn't see who it was. The footsteps came toward her and stopped behind her chair. The figure squatted down and grappled with the ropes binding her hands.

Who is it? Her mind tried to understand. "Umm uh um," she mumbled as loud as she could and shook her head.

The figure stood and reached for the knot on the gag. As it fell away, Ruth took a deep breath. "Thank you." She tried to peer at the figure. "Who are you?"

The figure stared at her silently, then mumbled a reply. "Jones." He squatted and went to work on the ropes holding her wrists.

"Mr. Jones, am I glad to see you! We have to hurry. Those two men were spies. Their boss will be here any minute, and then we're both in trouble."

He pulled and worked at the ropes, but the tight knots wouldn't budge.

"Get a knife from Suzi's drawer over there and cut them. Please hurry, Mr. Jones."

He brought the knife and bent to saw at the ropes. As the first one fell away, the door opened. Ruth's heart stopped, then pounded as if it would burst through her chest. Heavy footsteps entered the room, and a flashlight beamed its light, first on her and then on Mr. Jones as a large figure walked toward them.

"Why, Miss Sinclair, what are you doing here in these circumstances?" a voice inquired.

She peered toward the figure. That voice. Who. . .? "Oh, Mr. Owens," she exclaimed in relief, "I'm so glad it's you! Leland and his cousin are spies! Bert went to signal the boss! He'll be here any minute. We all need to get out of here as fast as we can!" She spoke rapidly as she stared at Herschel's dark figure.

Herschel ambled toward them. "Now, now, Miss Sinclair, don't you fret. You say there are spies around here? That's hard to believe, but maybe I should take a look. Mother always told me to be a good citizen. I'll just see if I can find out what they were up to, and then I'll take care of you." He walked directly to the bookshelves and searched through the titles.

"What are you doing way out here, Mr. Owens? It's so late." She watched his movements as his hand stopped on a book. His face looked eerie above the small beam of light directed toward the bookshelves.

"Why, I heard you had a nut harvest out here, Miss Sinclair. When the store closed, I came right over to see if I could help, but everyone appears to be gone."

An uneasy feeling rushed over her. *Why isn't he helping me first?* She watched as he picked up a book and looked through it, then walked to the table and peered at the Bible. He searched around, muttering angrily as he looked for something. How had he known where to look? How would he know about the book and the Bible? She gasped. No, it couldn't be!

"You're the boss!" she blurted out. "You're looking for Bert's codes!"

Herschel continued his search. "Now, Miss Sinclair, I'm deeply offended to have you accuse me like that. Mother would be so hurt if she knew you called *me* the boss." He slammed the book on the table.

As he searched frantically, his coat fell open, and she could see a gun tucked in his belt. She heard Mr. Jones catch his breath and stiffen behind her. He placed a hand on her shoulder and spoke up in his soft voice. "Saw Bert out at the pigeon coop when I come in. Might be he left something out there."

Herschel turned and the hard look on his face changed into his broad smile. "Why, I appreciate your help, sir. If I'm to solve this riddle, I need all the pieces. You both sit tight, and I'll be right back. Then I'll see to you." He gave Mr. Jones a hard look above the beam of light. Ruth could hear the scraping of wooden legs against the floor as he picked up a chair and slipped out the door. She heard him jamming the object under the handle on the outside of the door; then his footsteps faded away.

Mr. Jones quickly bent to saw at the ropes with Suzi's dull knife. Both froze as voices and shouts sounded outside. The door burst open, and they were instantly blinded by a mass of bright lights. In a flurry of activity, Ruth could make out men in police and military uniforms rushing about—and Carolyn Samuels. Ruth's head swirled as she tried to take it all in.

An officer hurried over and quickly cut the remaining ropes binding her. "Are you all right, miss?" She rubbed her wrists and nodded, then watched, confused, as Carolyn Samuels checked the table and bookcase carefully. Officers were searching the house, and she could hear others moving about outside.

"You do get in the biggest messes, Miss Sinclair." She heard that familiar voice behind her as Jim reached out to help her to her feet. "Are you okay?"

"Oh, Jim, I. . ." She longed to go to him for comfort—but there stood Carolyn Samuels, two feet away. Suddenly her legs felt weak, and she reached out to steady herself. She felt dazed and dizzy.

Jim grabbed her arm quickly. "Sit down. You've had quite a scare."

"The boss," she began. "He's out at the pigeon coop. It's Herschel Owens. Don't let him get away! He has some of the codes with him."

"The officers picked him up as he tried to escape in the dark," Jim reassured her.

Ruth looked around. "Where's Mr. Jones? He was helping me."

"Taking Tim and Charlie home. I'll explain later," Jim answered. "Right now these officers want a word with you. Then we need to get you home."

Two officers sat down at the table with Jim and Ruth, and Carolyn joined them. Jim introduced the officers. "And you've met Carolyn Samuels, government expert in codes and spies. She's been a big help." Ruth was so astounded she couldn't say a word. Carolyn smiled at her and shrugged.

"Now, Miss Sinclair, tell us what happened here today." The officer nodded to her, and the table was silent.

She took a deep breath and told all that had happened that afternoon. "Leland and Bert took off before you came," she added.

"I'll have our men out looking for them," the officer assured her and turned to speak to one of his men.

Jim shoved his chair back from the table. "She needs some rest, gentlemen," he said protectively. "This has been a rough day." He helped Ruth to her feet.

"We'll get in touch with you soon, miss. We'll have more questions," the officer said, "but they can hold till you've recovered. I—"

With a slam the door burst open, and George Peterson dashed into the room. "What's going on?" He looked around at the officers. "Why are all these men here? Ruth, are you okay? What's happened, Jim?" Fear and confusion showed on his face.

"Ruth's okay, Mr. Peterson," Jim assured him. "We caught one of the spies who had been using this place. Right now we have a lot of work to do here. Take Ruth home, if you would. I'll be tied up here for quite a while."

George shook his head. "Alma and I sat down to rest when Ruth left. We were so tired from the walnut picking we fell asleep in our chairs. When we woke up, it was dark and Ruth wasn't home yet so I hurried over here." He looked around at everyone. "It was only an hour or so."

Ruth came up and hugged her grandfather. She felt so safe tears finally came. George patted her shoulder. "I'm so sorry, Ruth. If anything. . ."

"I'm okay, Grandpa." She wiped her eyes and picked up the roast from the stove. "The Lord took care of me. Let's get home so Grandma won't worry." She paused at the door. "Thanks again to all of you."

&

As Ruth and George pulled into their driveway, Alma rushed

out to meet them. "Here's the roast, Gram. Now we can have dinner." Ruth handed her the roaster and got out of the car.

"Not till we find out what happened to you. We were so worried, Ruth." Alma followed her up the stairs.

Over a warm cup of cocoa Ruth related the afternoon's events. "Oh, Ruth, to think. . . The Lord was good." Alma stood up. "Now to bed with you. We'll talk more after you've recovered."

twenty-one

The bedroom was dark when Ruth awoke. She sat up quickly in confusion. "What day is this?" She shook her head to chase away the cobwebs. "Why is my room still dark? Isn't it morning?"

Slowly her thoughts began to clear, and the frightening events came flooding back. "Oh, no," she said aloud, "it can't be true." She reached over to turn on the lamp beside her bed. Ten o'clock! She stared at the alarm clock on her dresser. "It's still Saturday, and all these terrible things happened only a few hours ago? Or was it just a nightmare?"

Grandma and Grandpa will know, she assured herself and headed for the stairs.

Below she could hear voices that sounded like Jim talking to George and Alma in the kitchen. Words and phrases drifted up to her. "Spies. . .Herschel. . ." Jim's voice faded, then returned. "Carolyn. . ." he was saying. "Worked together closely. . .engaged. . .friend. . .Ruth."

She grabbed the stair rail to steady herself and sank down on a step. *So that's the way it is. The nightmare did happen, and Jim and Carolyn are engaged.* She tried to breathe, but her chest was tight with a terrible ache. She couldn't seem to catch her breath. *All this in one day! How. . .? How can I. . .?*

All her hopes and fears and dreams jumbled about in the turmoil inside her. As the ache in her chest threatened to stifle her, she bowed her head. "Lord," she whispered, "this is so hard, but You saved me this afternoon. I know I can trust You with my life. And I know You have a purpose for me, whether it's with someone else someday or teaching children. I'll always have You." She took a deep breath. "If it's Your will for Jim and Carolyn to be together, I trust You and ask You to bless them and to heal the ache in my heart." A quiet peace settled over her.

She sat there a moment. "Lord, I've been a slow learner when it comes to trust. And it took something terrible to teach me." She nodded. "Jim was right when he said You often get a lot done in the bad times." She got up and headed down the stairs.

"Having a party without me?" she quipped as she walked into the kitchen. George and Jim rushed to pull out a chair for her. "Here, sit, Ruth," George said as he grabbed her elbow. "Jim's been telling us what happened."

A plate of roast beef sandwiches sat in the middle of the table. "We never did get around to having supper tonight. After all the trouble you went through, I thought we could at least have sandwiches." Alma passed the plate to her. "Here, Ruth. You need to keep up your strength."

"They look delicious, Gram," Ruth said as she reached for one.

"We feel so bad we fell asleep and didn't come looking for you sooner." Alma placed a cup of tea in front of Ruth.

"The Lord took care of me. Someone could have been hurt if Grandpa had burst in earlier." She smiled calmly and took a sip of tea.

"I came over tonight to see if there's more information you three can give us." Jim stared at his cup and turned it in his hand. "You know the most about what's been going on. We're hoping you can add some missing pieces so we can get this cleared up." He looked up at them sharply. "Whatever we say here tonight is not to leave this room. I hope you understand."

The three nodded.

"Wartime necessity," George agreed.

"Good." Jim sat back. "Now that you've had a rest, Ruth, tell me again what happened today, especially what Bert did and in what order."

Ruth recounted the evening, then paused to think. "About Bert. As I remember, first he took a tiny piece of paper from his pocket, and Leland brought him another that came in a capsule the pigeons had carried. Then he turned to someplace in the Bible and wrote on one of Suzi's bookmarks. I think that's the one that fell under the table."

"We found it," Jim said.

"He took *Ben-Hur* and underlined words in it, then wrote on another bookmark. Oh, yes, there was a strip of paper with some writing on it, too." She looked over at Jim. "What's it all about?"

"Carolyn thinks they were attempting a complicated communication system so no one could tell what they were doing," Jim explained. "The Nakamuras were religious and liked to read, so the material was all there—and with the pigeons they were all set to send and receive information. Our experts are working to figure it out. Shouldn't be too hard. They weren't geniuses." Jim took a sip of the tea. "We do know Bert and Leland were part of the mob that ransacked the Nakamuras' house. They must have seen the possibilities and passed the idea on to the boss."

"The boss!" Ruth sat up straight. "Was I shocked to find out it was Herschel! I'm so glad you got him."

Jim smiled. "We caught Herschel Owens and the boss, but Bert and Leland are long gone. Leland didn't even take his things. Just ran. Bert must have seen the police descend on the place. He's gone, too."

Ruth nodded. "It figures. Leland was really scared when he found out spies could be executed or sent to prison." She frowned. "But what did you mean, they caught Herschel Owens and the boss? Herschel was the boss."

"That's what we thought at first, too," Jim said, "but when the officers searched Trader's Corner, they found the whole setup and the identity of the real boss—his mother!"

Ruth sat back astounded. "His mother!" She nodded slowly. "Yes, it makes sense. I always said she'd be more at home running a chain gang than being the loving mother Herschel talked about."

"This isn't the first trouble she's been in," Jim added. "The government's been looking for her for several years."

"Oh, my!" Alma exclaimed. "I hardly knew her, but here in our own community. . ."

"Those two had quite a racket going. In the storeroom they were getting ready to print counterfeit ration books to sell. The furniture store, if you call it that, was just a front for their various illegal activities," Jim explained.

"That fits. Leland told me Bert was the best counterfeiter around." Ruth finished her tea and set the cup down.

George leaned forward. "Every time Ruth and I went to Nakamuras's we found a different number of pigeons. They took 'em to send messages, appears to me." He went on to explain what he and Ruth had seen at the pigeon coop over the months.

"You're right, Mr. Peterson. We found pigeon droppings all over their storeroom."

"Why did they tear up all those bookcases and Ruth's room?" Alma looked puzzled. "What does that have to do with this?"

Jim shifted his chair as Ruth got up to pour more tea. "It appears Herschel and his mother were hoping to sell information about our war production and used Bert and Leland to collect it. The pigeons brought the Bible references that gave Bert messages from the boss, Carolyn assumes, and then Bert relayed their information through words he designated in *Ben-Hur*. She thinks the bookmark and the strip of paper had master codes written on them."

"Remember the bookmark I found under the sofa cushion, Ruth?" Alma asked. "The one with the chapters and verse numbers not in the Bible? That must have been one of the code lists."

Ruth poured the tea. "The boss was desperate to get the book and bookmark back because they were incriminating evidence. Bert tore up my room even though the book was lying on the bed because he also needed the bookmark with coding on it." She sat down and related the rest of Leland's ramblings that afternoon. "And Bert was the one who could break in anywhere. He used a skeleton key to open the Nakamuras's door."

"But looks like they got careless sometimes. Left the door open and even let Fluffy get caught inside," George commented.

"I don't understand. If Bert and Leland hate foreigners so much, why would they help them by spying?" Alma looked puzzled.

"They wanted money," Ruth explained. "They worked for the boss and didn't see themselves as part of the war or helping either side, just themselves. They were anti-Japanese and tried to use that to keep us away from the house. When it didn't work, they went ahead anyway." A memory came back to her. "Mr. Jones. He was trying to help me when you came, Jim. I want to thank him."

Jim smiled and looked over at her. "You have three heroes to thank."

Ruth frowned. "Three heroes? I don't understand."

Jim sat back in his chair. "Tim and Charlie were down at the creek, building a raft, late that afternoon. Old man—er—Mr. Jones was helping them. The three had become good friends and worked together on the project. Mr. Jones came up to Nakamuras' to find a rope they needed to secure the raft for the night. When he went by the window, he saw you with Bert and Leland."

"That was the face we saw!" Ruth exclaimed.

Jim nodded. "He knew those two had caused trouble before, so he went back to get the boys. The three hurried to check out the situation. You heard their footsteps on the porch. Mr. Jones sent the boys to tell me you were in trouble while he stayed to keep an eye on things."

"But when Bert checked, no one was there." Ruth was puzzled.

"They ducked under the porch. He didn't look there. Bert and Leland aren't the brightest. I called various authorities right away. We arrived in the dark and saw a flashlight over at the pigeon coop where we picked up Herschel. Then we came to find you."

George shook his head. "I should have taken it more seriously when Ruth told me about the strange goings-on, but the sheriff wouldn't listen, and there was nothing else to do."

"The sheriff has a problem with an anti-Japanese attitude, so he didn't really care what happened over there—or to any of their friends," Jim explained.

Alma sighed and sat back. "Now that you're safe, Ruth, I'm suddenly very tired. It's been a hard day. Ready for some sleep, George?"

"Don't have to ask me twice. My back's letting me know I did too much bending for a man my age." He stood. "The Lord's been good to us today." He patted Ruth's shoulder tenderly as he left the room.

Ruth poured two more cups of tea. "Thanks for all you did, Jim. I have so many questions, I don't know where to begin." She took a sip of the hot tea and set the cup down.

Jim was quiet.

And I know why, she thought, *but I'm at peace with it. I trust the Lord's plan for each of us.*

Jim finally looked up. "Ruth, I'm not sure where to begin. This has gotten so tangled."

"It's okay, Jim, I know. . ."

He reached out and put his hand on hers. "Let me explain. Please. There's still much I'm not allowed to say, so I have to choose my words carefully, but you deserve the best explanation I can give. I'll probably say more than I should." He paused and considered his words.

"You knew I worked with my dad at the plant," he began. "What you didn't know is how I'm, uh, also connected with the government. Since I couldn't get in the service, I became involved with other departments that have to do with national security. The plant was not only a good cover for my special activities but also useful to the war effort. We knew Swan Island Shipyards could become a target for spy efforts, along with any converted industry like our plant. As community coordinator I'd be in a good spot to keep a handle on things. And here on the West Coast we had to get defense efforts going as soon as possible."

Ruth was surprised. "I had no idea, Jim. I just thought. . ."

He nodded. "You were the last person I wanted to put in danger, so the less you knew the better, and all this had to stay quiet. We wanted to get the big guys behind the scenes, not just the small fish like Bert and Leland." He lowered his head and shook it. "Then I messed up big-time."

Her eyebrows went up. "Were you in danger?" she asked with concern.

"Not the way you mean, but my whole future was in jeopardy." He put both hands around hers. "Ruth, I know about Harold and what happened. You can't imagine how terrible I felt."

"No, Jim, it's. . ."

"Shh." He squeezed her hands. "Let me explain. We needed to get Carolyn Samuels into the Fir Glen community without raising suspicion. She's highly trained in detecting spies and breaking codes. So when they suggested she pose as my girlfriend, I went along with it. You were still being loyal to Harold. I thought it might make you jealous." He looked at her sheepishly.

Ruth's mouth fell open, and she sat speechless.

"Only a couple of weeks later I learned the truth about Harold, but by then they couldn't let me out of the plan."

"You mean you're not engaged?"

"Engaged? Where'd you get that idea?"

"When I came down the stairs a while ago, I heard you talking to Grandma and Grandpa about Carolyn and being engaged."

He let out a breath. "Carolyn's engaged—but not to me. To a guy overseas."

"Then you mean. . ."

"I mean I'm not attached in any way to anyone—yet. Now I'm afraid I'll never be. I'm afraid I've blown it with you completely." He glanced at her sideways. "I'm afraid to hope."

He looked miserable. "I've been in love with you ever since I helped you out of the mud in Nakamuras' driveway last spring and now. . ." He shook his head hopelessly.

She caught her breath and sat up, trying to grasp his words. The room was silent, and the clock ticked loudly as relief washed over her. She straightened in her chair and looked over at Jim. "I will say this has affected our friendship, Jim," she said with as serious an expression as she could manage. "As you recall, we're just friends unless. . ." She raised an eyebrow at him.

He sat there, not sure he had heard right. He blinked and looked up as he caught her meaning. Then he leaned back in his chair, that mischievous smile spreading over his face as he took a deep breath in relief.

"So, Miss Sinclair," he teased, "you're not engaged?"

She shook her head.

"No commitments?"

"None."

"You've promised to wait for someone?"

"No, sir."

"Then one more thing we have to clear up. Do I have to take you out on a first date before I ask you to marry me?" The old Jim was back. "With a war on, there's no time to wait on formalities."

"No moonlight and roses?" she teased back.

He stood and held out his hand. "My lady, would you do me the honor of accompanying me on a date to your grandparents' living room? The moon's not out tonight, and the rose season has passed, but I have many sweet nothings to whisper in your ear."

Ruth stood and gave a small curtsy. "Offer accepted, sir." She took his arm. They walked to the living room and sat down on the sofa. He put his arm around her and pulled her close.

"Remember the old high school rule, Jim. No kiss till the third date."

"Since you're already home on date one, I'll ask you out on

dates two and three right now."

"I accept," she murmured as he lifted her chin and kissed her. She caught her breath and nestled in his arms as all the months of heartache melted away.

Jim stroked her hair. "Someday I'd like to shake the hand of the woman who ran off with Harold."

She touched his face tenderly. "You already had my heart, Jim, but I'm glad we don't have to wait till Harold comes home," she agreed.

"So, if I promise to protect you from spies, keep your bookcases safe, and never buy you pigeons, will you marry me, Ruth Sinclair?"

She gazed into the love in his eyes. "Yes, Jim, spies and all." His tender kiss left her weak and breathless.

"So, how about tomorrow?"

She frowned. "Tomorrow for what?"

"To get married, of course. With the war, everything's escalated, so no use wasting time here either."

"Oh, no, Jim Griffin, there may be a war on, but you're not depriving this girl of time to plan the big day!" She smiled at him sweetly. "Speaking of plans, we have a lot to talk about—like what date and our colors." She excitedly chattered on about ideas for the wedding and their life together. "Of course Pastor Cameron will marry us."

Jim shook his head. "Women. . ."

A loud crash in the kitchen sent a bolt of fear through both of them. Jim froze for an instant before he dashed to the kitchen. Sounds of hurrying footsteps came from her grandparents' hall.

"What's going on?" George switched on the light as they rushed into the room.

The four of them stared at the table. There stood Fluffy with a piece of roast beef in her mouth, a broken plate, and sandwich remains on the floor.

"How in the world did you get in here?" Alma demanded of the cat.

Jim took a deep breath. "That may have been my fault," he said sheepishly. "When I came over tonight she was by the door. I didn't pay any attention to her as I came in. She must have sneaked by."

George nodded. "We were too worried about other things to notice."

"Now that you two are up," Jim began, "I have something to discuss with you. Since Ruth's parents aren't here, Mr. Peterson, I'll ask you for Ruth's hand in marriage. And I warn you, sir, I won't take no for an answer."

Alma's hand flew to her face. "Oh, my, thank You, Lord. You've answered my prayer!"

George beamed and reached out to shake Jim's hand. "With pleasure. You have our blessings, Son."

Alma hugged them both. "When is the big event?"

"Tomorrow morning?" Jim suggested hopefully.

Ruth wrinkled her nose at him and rolled her eyes. "Men!" She looked at Alma. "December will be best, don't you think? Mom and Dad will be home for that month."

"That's such a short time. There's so much to do," Alma said. "We'll have to. . ."

George interrupted. "Get used to it, Jim. The women are taking over already. Time for some sleep, Alma. Leave the planning to them." George put his arm around her shoulder and turned her toward the hall. He stopped. "Housing's tight these days. You always have a home with us if you need it."

Ruth looked at Jim. "We talked about it and decided we'll stay at the Nakamuras' for now. Suzi would be so pleased, and we can keep a better eye on the place."

Alma gave Ruth a hug. "The Lord knew what was right for you." She looked fondly at her granddaughter. "The best I can wish is that you be as happy as I've been."

George beamed and gave a cocky strut. "These women sure know how to find the best, Jim." He winked at him and sashayed down the hall.

"That man!" Alma declared. "I thank the Lord you're as

blessed as I am, Ruth."

When they were alone, Jim took her hands. "This was not planned for tonight. I don't have a ring to give you."

"As long as I have your heart, that's all I need." She reached up and kissed him tenderly.

"I'd like to announce this in church tomorrow. I'm taking no chances on your backing down."

She laughed. "Don't worry. You're stuck, Jim Griffin. There's no getting out of this now!"

❧

The next morning the four entered the church and found a pew. At the end of the service, Pastor Cameron paused and looked out over the congregation. "We have some joyous news to share this morning. Jim Griffin will tell you about it."

Jim stood and pulled Ruth to her feet. "I need to finish something I started, and what better place than among God's people. Last night I asked Ruth to marry me. It wasn't planned, so I didn't have a ring."

Across the room Marge let out a gasp.

He reached in his pocket. "Ruth, in front of these dear people of God, will you accept this ring and build a life with God and me?" He slipped a beautiful old-fashioned ring on her finger. "It was my grandmother's."

Her heart was so full all she could do was nod. Tears came to her eyes as she beamed at him.

Friends quickly milled about them, offering congratulations. Marge pushed her way through the crowd. "I'm so happy for you!" She hugged Ruth. "And you've saved my reputation. I'm a matchmaking success, after all!"

"You need to circle our date on your calendar, Marge. I'm counting on you to be my maid of honor."

"You bet! I never dreamed you'd beat me to the altar, though!"

As the congratulations ebbed, Ruth saw Tim, Charlie, and Mr. Jones standing at the side of the room. She pulled Jim by the hand and went over to them.

"Hey, Miss Sinclair, we helped solve the mystery," Tim whispered. "But we're not supposed to tell. War secrets, you know. Maybe we'll get a medal when the war's over."

Charlie beamed and nodded.

Ruth patted Tim's shoulder. "You probably saved my life, boys. Jim and I thank you with all our hearts."

She turned to Mr. Jones. He was dressed neatly in an old-fashioned suit. She held out her hand. "Thank you, sir," was all she could say. She squeezed his hand tightly.

"Suzi was good to me. I look out for her friends and her place," he said with a slight bow. He glanced at Tim and Charlie. "They're my friends."

"We brought him here, Miss Sinclair. He doesn't know much God stuff, but we're teaching him. I told him about David and Goliath."

Charlie nodded.

"We're proud of you boys." Jim smiled at them and ruffled Tim's hair.

"Let's go." Jim directed Ruth toward the door.

They stepped out of the church and headed for the parking lot. Jim got in the car beside Ruth. "I'm taking you to dinner to celebrate, Miss Sinclair." He reached for her left hand. "Mm, that ring looks good on your finger. Too bad all our parents are out of town on business. Mine were thrilled when we called them. Mom was the one who suggested I use Grandma's ring." He paused. "But if you want a new one all your own, we can look tomorrow."

"No way! You're never getting this one off my finger, Jim Griffin."

Jim drummed his fingers on the steering wheel as he waited for a car to pass, then pulled out onto the road. "I have a question." He paused a moment. "You went through a terrible scare yesterday, then thought I was engaged to Carolyn. Yet when you came into the kitchen, you were so calm and at peace. What happened?"

Ruth stared out the window and smiled. "The Lord looked

out for my life yesterday afternoon. I let go and trusted Him with my heart and my future, too." She looked over at him. "Remember Pastor Cameron's victory sermon the first Sunday you came to church last spring?"

"Hmm, so you noticed me way back then?" He nodded and grinned. "I was hoping you fell for me the day we met."

Ruth rolled her eyes at him. "When I thought you were engaged, I sat down on the steps and let God have control of my life. And I had peace." She smiled. "I like the phrase Pastor Cameron used—'C for victory.' That's where peace comes from—not from winning wars or getting our own way but from Christ's victory in our hearts."

Jim nodded and squeezed her hand.

He pulled into the restaurant parking lot. "Ready, Mrs. Griffin? I wanted to hear how it sounded."

"Mm, I like it."

He opened the door and took her hand. "Just want you to get used to it. That'll be your name for at least the next fifty years!"

A Letter To Our Readers

Dear Reader:

In order that we might better contribute to your reading enjoyment, we would appreciate your taking a few minutes to respond to the following questions. We welcome your comments and read each form and letter we receive. When completed, please return to the following:

Rebecca Germany, Fiction Editor
Heartsong Presents
PO Box 719
Uhrichsville, Ohio 44683

1. Did you enjoy reading *C for Victory?*
   ☐ Very much. I would like to see more books
      by this author!
   ☐ Moderately
      I would have enjoyed it more if _____

   _____

   _____

2. Are you a member of **Heartsong Presents**? Yes ☐ No ☐
   If no, where did you purchase this book? _____

   _____

3. How would you rate, on a scale from 1 (poor) to 5 (superior), the cover design? _____

4. On a scale from 1 (poor) to 10 (superior), please rate the following elements.

   _____ Heroine   _____ Plot

   _____ Hero   _____ Inspirational theme

   _____ Setting   _____ Secondary characters

5. These characters were special because_____

    _____

    _____

6. How has this book inspired your life?_____

    _____

    _____

7. What settings would you like to see covered in future
    Heartsong Presents books?_____

    _____

    _____

8. What are some inspirational themes you would like to see
    treated in future books?_____

    _____

    _____

9. Would you be interested in reading other **Heartsong
    Presents** titles?   Yes ❑   No ❑

10. Please check your age range:
    ❑ Under 18   ❑ 18-24   ❑ 25-34
    ❑ 35-45   ❑ 46-55   ❑ Over 55

11. How many hours per week do you read?_____

Name _____

Occupation _____

Address _____

City _____ State _____ Zip _____